Impostor Baby Mama

A book of comedy by **Mark Flame** – *The brain of the game*

A Sky Master Production

For enquiries contact Mark Flame: elsuej@gmail.com

Just *laugh!*

Life is too serious

To take

Seriously!!!

Rochelle Benson was a lucky woman. She had the perfect husband in Benny. Then Olive Oil looking Betsy Frazier brought a boy that seemed identical to her son, claiming that Benny Benson was the father!

You could not judge a book by the cover and you could not substitute the look of a child for a DNA test. Benny went to prove that point. Simple ABC could not possibly go wrong! So...how come shit happened?

Prologue

She sat for hours waiting for her favorite radio show to begin at 11:45. Tonight's topic was about star children born as jewels in their parents' crowns. The young West Keyes Island sprint sensation Benny Benson was a prime example. Most people picked him to challenge the masterful Usain Bolt at some point in his career. Benjy joked that it was impossible as Usain was 'a Bolt'.

Simon laughed and chipped in, "Talking about Benny! At his young age he does incredibly well financially. He has never been to the Olympics yet ladies and gentlemen! You won't make millions as a junior in a country like Jamaica if you can't show an actual 'senior' world class medal. That would be the ordinary. Benny is the best West Keyes has ever done! He is our star and he sells! Put his name on ugly and it's off the shelf!"

"Well," Benjy interjected, "Let's remind our listeners that Benny is preparing for his first Olympics. Since he was not running with the seniors, he could not win senior medals! He's training hard and coming up to speed! He's stashing up the medals on the junior level both here and on the international circles. It's clear to see what's coming later on! Will he be Bolt's nemesis?"

"That's true Benjy. I don't know that any junior athlete in any country would be buying his parents a luxury home and a BMW!"

"That is to show you Simon! This kid is the biggest brand on the island. West Keyes citizens spend their money! Still, what Benny does in our country, Bolt does anywhere in the world! He'll pack a stadium for you in a

bolt. But let's get back to the topic! Imagine just having a kid, being a good parent working hard and bruising your knuckles off. Then all of a sudden this kid takes the world in his hand and you are having coffee with bank managers and driving in limousines! What a way to say 'thanks for bringing me into the world'! That's the story of Benny Benson and the Benson family!"

"It is the story of Usain Bolt too!"

"Yes, I read some article. Nice story!"

"Nice story? It's a freaking fairy tale! Let's go to the phone and get our lovely listeners to join in the discussion. We are talking about star children that come to this earth. All their parents had to do was own them, be good parents and BOOM – They were rich!"

Simon made his customary laugh and said his usual words. "It's going to be a beautiful night talking with you people. How do I know? Because Simon says so!"

The phone rang…

"Hello!" said Simon, "You're the first caller on The Greatness of Sports tonight. I'm Simon Dunbar. Who's calling?"

"Hello! It's me!" the caller announced, expecting everyone to know her.

Simon said, "Tell me who is 'you' so I will know."

"I won't keep you guessing then! I'm Betsy Frazier, your biggest fan!"

"Is this your first time calling Betsy Frazier?"

"Yes Simon. It is!"

"That's why I could not guess who it was. I didn't know you! What's on your mind tonight Betsy?"

"I'm calling to find out where to find Usain Bolt!"

Simon stuttered and then asked. "Can I ask why you'd ask that question?"

"Yes. Because I'm a fan of his and I deserve to have access to him!"

"That's it?"

"Yes! That's it. I want my son to buy me one BMW!"

"I hope he does! How old is he?"

"He's not born yet. I haven't contacted his father!"

"Oh! I see you have a funny bone in you! You're picking up on the 'Boom you're rich line', right?"

"Yes! So where is Usain Bolt?"

Simon laughed and his colleague joined in. Betsy was the joker but she was not laughing. When they were done she asked matter-of-factually, "So, where is he?"

Simon chuckled, "Unfortunately, we wouldn't know where to find him! Usain Bolt lives in Jamaica. That's well out of your way! Maybe Benny will make a better shot; give him a year or two!" He laughed and Benji was cracking up!

"Wow! Why don't these athletes make themselves accessible? Do they think that fans come cheap?"

She paused. Simon chuckled and waited to see if she would pop another one.

"Well, how about Justin Gatlin?" she asked.

This time the men could hardly stop laughing. "What?" Simon finally caught his breath enough to ask.

"How about Justin Gatlin? Is he in Jamaica too?"

"No! He lives in America! Another hard one!"

"It's damned unfair!"

"I know!" Simon chuckled, "By the way Betsy, how old are you?"

"Very young! I'm thirty nine and my eggs are kicking!"

He guffawed, "It seems you're running out of time!"

"I never…"

The timer buzzed. Simon informed her reluctantly. "Betsy! I have to go! The lines are blowing up with people! Bye now! Call back next week!"

Betsy put the phone down and shook her head. A light bulb lit up in her cranium! All she had to do was be a good parent! BOOM – She would be rich!

"Silly Simon talking about I'm running out of time! I'm still young! My son is going to buy me a luxury home!"

It was not easy to get to prospective dads overseas. A Jamaican girl once said that if you could not catch Quawko you could catch his shirt! Usain Bolt was running with his shirt trailing behind him. That would be 'Benny Benson'!

"Boom!" she said, cackling. "I'm rich!"

1

Three years later…

Someone was coming down the corridor. Cassandra's lips curled spitefully. Jennifer saw the look on her face and questioned, "Who?"

She giggled impulsively, watching Jennifer's stupefied expression. "If you guessed that it's the boogie woman you're right!" Cassandra replied disgustedly. "By the look on your face, I know you suspected it!"

Jennifer winced. "*Ewe*! It's the ultimate be-grudger! Why is she working today?"

"She shouldn't be! But she's here looking like Popeye's Olive Oil, *'styling'* and stepping like she's hot!"

Cassandra cackled. "The only part of her that's hot is her underprivileged punaany! Fishermen won't hook up that nook and it can't entice a fisherman!"

"*I know*! Like it or not, the frenemy is here!"

"God doesn't like ugly Jennifer! She's damned ugly inside and it shows outside! She's *every* ugly!"

"Years ago there were ugly people and pretty people. Now there are only pretty people and people that can't be bothered. She can't be bothered to have a clean mind and she can't be bothered to even wash her hair or buy some proper make up! People are ugly by choice Cassandra."

Jennifer was about to speak again. Cassandra cautioned her. Betsy Frazier was in the hearing range!

From inside the room the sound of Betsy's heels on the tiles were loud. She did that clumsy, ugly and overcooked walk! How revolting! Even as it would repulse her, curiosity drew Jennifer outside the room to the passageway. She stood beside her best friend to sweat out the unpleasant experience.

Jennifer cupped her palms to Cassandra's right ear, "She's trying to be *you*! She's dying to get laid but she's doing a cock dropping walk! Can't she be herself? *Jeepers*! Walking like a fucking milk laden mother goat!"

Cassandra returned the favor, "Old maid thinks she's young! Hear her shoes going *floppily-flop cock drop*!"

Betsy came closer. Cassandra's deep distasteful look morphed into mocked acceptance. She touched Jennifer compelling her to shape-shift too. They pooled together for courage to turn their efforts into plastic smiles.

The pretty women concealed the antipathy but only for professional reasons. Betsy had a predilection for feistiness. They had no recourse but to be subjective!

On several occasions, they got spoken to for dissenting. Twice they were suspended for not relenting after being warned. Punishment was pain in their pockets. They had to refrain from the fisticuffs. Betsy kept coming to seek their worship. It was aggravating!

Before *'The Evil'* came, the room service manager was one of them! Mrs. Harrison used to be a proud beauty too. She had a glamorous ring on her finger to prove it. A year after landing *'Mr. Money'*, she became too good for everyone else but Betsy. She used to help them to fend her off. Now, suddenly, *she would not tolerate intolerance, bullying and petty prejudices.*

That prescribed injustice forced them to embrace and tolerate *'The Anti-Beauty'*! She was *'Double Ugly'*, for she was ugly inside and outside! She was *'Every Ugly'* because she was spiritually and physically ugly. Even her Christianity was grimy!

Their repulsion coupled with the demand for open-mindedness crossbred into a bedeviled look on their faces. It came with hard practice but they managed to skin their teeth and force on plastic smiles for Betsy, which made them feel like mannequins.

Betsy Frazier darned near owned them! She owned their boss too! Anyone who labeled her the victim knew nothing! The only advantage this rogue duo had was to call her ugly names. That was a huge step down from physically putting her through the shredder!

Betsy stepped to her gorgeous coworkers and subjects. On seeing their wonderful smiles of approval she put more flavor into her steps. She wanted to believe they appreciated and admired her and that their stitched on smiles served to prove it. Betsy envisioned Cassandra walking and stepped to mirror the picture-perfect image. They were two beautiful women. She determined to be the compatible number three.

"Praise Jesus sisters! It's *me*!" Betsy announced excitedly. The stupefied duo nodded fake approvals. They were overly unimpressed with being her 'sisters'.

"I see it's you," Jennifer suggested matter of factually. "I didn't know you were working today."

"Yeah!" Cassandra added, "It's your day off, Betsy!"

Betsy smiled mischievously, "Mrs. Harrison wanted *me* to do Room B 17. Then I'll be done for the day!"

Jennifer frowned, "*Why*? What's special in there? It's the same job! It can't be freaking rocket science!"

Betsy graced them with her most noble look. Then she applied that air of godlike indulgence to lesser beings. "Y'all don't know? *Oh, I'm sorry – You wouldn't!*"

"What don't we know?" Cassandra inquired edgily.

"The *honeymooners* are in there!"

"What honeymooners Betsy?" Jennifer chipped in with incredulity. "There are always honeymooners in half the rooms in this hotel!"

Betsy grinned with an ace. "Not *Benny Benson*!"

At that revealing the beauties turned to each other with hysterical orgasmic shock. Then they performed the synchronized emotional scream of disbelief. *"Who?"*

"The Benny Benson is in there!"

They heard rumors that Benny and Rochelle were planning a second honey moon six months after their wedding. They vented their excitement begrudging the fact that the news came by the mouth of their anti-beauty nemesis. Benny Benson came on her day off! She worked her evil to take away their opportunity to do his room! By her privilege, she would be up in there until he checked out!

Mrs. Harrison was biased. Betsy wanted to meet the celebrity so they did not matter!

"Why the boss didn't tell us?" Jennifer questioned.

Betsy delightfully spoke words to induce more hate. "Jean cannot trust just *anyone*! Benny will be upset if everyone knows where he's spending his honeymoon."

Cassandra griped, "Is that so?"

Betsy strutted around in half a circle, drawing attention to the finesse that won her the privilege. Then she said, "*Yes* girls! She had to make sure I did that room to guarantee the guest's satisfaction."

"I've been working here longer than you and no guest was ever dissatisfied with me!" Jennifer agitated.

"Me too!" Cassandra added raising her left palm, "We've been professionals here until today! Benny had better watch out for you! You have an evil agenda!"

"Yes!" Jennifer chipped in, "You're evil posing as good like the Pope of Rome!"

"For your information," Betsy snapped back, taking on her devil's demeanor, "Benny Benson is very impressed with me and the Pope of Rome represents God on earth! You're both devils!"

"She thinks a cross-dressing man in a skirt named 'the panty fits' has authority on godhood!" Cassandra poked spitefully – Not to insult the Pope but to get under Betsy's skin. She was absolutely dumb in their eyes and when she was agitated she got dumber still.

"Stupid *blasphemers*! You don't even know titles! It's not *'the panty fits'*! It's 'the Pontiff'! And it's no skirt either! It's a robe, like what Jesus wore! You're dumb!"

Jennifer giggled "Leave Jesus out of it please!" Then she asked "Did Benny say he was impressed with you or did you just add a lie as the good Christian you are?"

Betsy blinked and took on her dignified posture. "*Yes*! Benny said I was the best – one dozen times and gave me a hug! He tips greatly too! Christians know how to please him! Bad people badmouth Christians but they will burn in hell!"

"That's a lie!" Cassandra refuted. *"Bad people* badmouth logical people and good mouth the religious! *Good people* say what is true about disgusting fake Christians! *You* don't like it because the culprit is you! You are a deceiving devil! Even if the bible says 'the skirt of his garment' you will still insist that it's not a skirt! God is going to light fire on you first!"

"I'm a good Christian! You had no right to blaspheme against the Pope and Jesus!"

Cassandra retorted matter of factually, "I did not blaspheme against Jesus – *You holy liar father fucker*! I blasphemed against the Pope! He deserves it! His organization blasphemes little boys' butts all day!"

"Preach!" Jennifer confirmed like a zealous witness, "You brought Jesus' name into the matter, Betsy! You tried to bring him low like the panty fitting Pope!"

"I call on his name because I'm highly blessed and highly favored! And, since you don't know, the Pope belongs to Jesus! Jesus will burn you in Hell!"

"Jesus takes too long to figure you out! He made the same mistake with Judas!"

The girls did not just up and hate the Be-grudger for no reason. They hated her and all she stood for – to even the church she attended and the religion she chose! Only gravity saved them from disrespecting Jesus for her sake. At times, even by his name, she coined the rhetoric that insulted their integrities. Jesus could cast her out of his midst long before, but he did not! That gave them a bone to pick at him too, just as they had one to pick at Mrs. Harrison for switching sides.

She took and owned their friend Jean. Now Betsy was working them over. She wanted to see them yield to her superior air so she could feel like somebody.

For the umpteenth time since working at Clair-Castle, her move to draw worship backfired! She saw their faces the instant the dam burst! Unsustainable hate broke from the shackles of professionalism to the gutters of informal grime. She knew these girls were able warriors! Betsy Frazier was a courageous fool!

"*Oops!*" she lamented, but in a matter of factual way, seeing that she overdid it. She would be abused! She prayed it would not include the fisticuffs.

The first time they succumbed to the rage, Fay, the Jamaican saved her from the shredder. Surprisingly, Fay reprimanded her saying, "Stop looking for trouble scrawny gal! They will bust your bombo-claat! Next time I won't save your raas like I am Jeezus Chris'! Cassandra and Jennifer don't play! I wouldn't fuck with them! I'm allergic to kicks and thumps! Seems you come to work to get bitch licks!"

It was obvious who Fay blamed for the trouble. Ungrateful as it were, Betsy made sure that the Jamaican got suspended for indecent language and verbal abuse. Fay returned a week later still set in her ways and not paying the respect she should.

Mrs. Harrison called Fay to reprimand her again, with Betsy as the complainant. To their utter shock, the

Jamaican took over the meeting determined to show them *'verbal abuse'*! She was armed and dangerous!

Fay ended by saying "Go away fiddle foot dry womb dry pussy old Betsy who thinks she's young! Stop envying young greasy girls! And you whoring manager Jean Harrison! Talking about you're charging me for *verbal abuse* and you giving your husband emotional abuse! You sold out your husband's pride! Go retrieve Mr. Harrison's back-shot that you gave away in Room B 17! Conman took his marital back shot gone to Trinidad! *Read my lips*! Buy a ticket, go bring it back and leave me alone! You understand?"

Jean blinked at Fay and then blinked at the wall. Fay waited for her to confirm her understanding of the instructions. Betsy tried to put on an innocent face but it made her look guilty. Fay eyed the pen that Jean was about to write her up with. It fell from the managers grasp, useless on the table. Fay nodded comprehendingly. Then she rose, went out and closed the door quietly behind her.

The meeting was over! Mrs. Harrison was shocked. An insensitive Jamaican worker knew and revealed her privates like news to her! Betsy watched grudgingly as Fay fell through the crack. She could not win! She hated fucking unbending Jamaicans! This was not the first one she met who would neither bend forward nor backward! Stiff necked people?

Betsy reached out to comfort her manager. "Oh Jean! She's so dumb! How can anyone take back a back shot? It's done and gone! Just give your hussy a different one! You got the infinity! *Duh!*"

Harrison was not amused! She watched Betsy with utter betrayal. Betsy shook her head to say she did not know how Fay got the ammunition. Jean did not believe her but she was telling the truth.

"Instead of us both worrying about *Harry's* back shot, as if I'm the only one who got *instructions*," Jean agitated, "Why don't *I* worry about *Harry's* back shot and *you* worry about *your* fiddle foot, dry womb and dry pussy? *Comprehend?*"

Jamaicans said that bushes had ears. A Jamaican worker proved it! Bushes indeed spoke to Moses, so there! Room B 17 was not in the bush but 'the bush' was compromised in room B 17 by way of an unholy undignified back-shot. The moral of the parable was very much relevant in this case...

Back in the moment, Betsy watched Cassandra and Jennifer, hoping all would defuse. They froze, half-amused at her reaction to her own insolence. She could not help admiring how beautiful they looked even while being pissed off. Then she went back to heart-pounding tension. Everything froze in that moment of suspense before flaming tongues unleashed upon her! Jennifer started with "*Every Ugly Olive Oil*!"

Betsy defended "Hah! Olive's not real! It's a Popeye cartoon!"

Cassandra added "Anti-Beauty *old foot bitch*!"

"Don't call me that Cassandra James! I'm not *old*!"

"Betsy Ugly Bones Dried Old Punaany Frazier?"

"I'll have you know that mine is wetter than yours! You'll see who the dried up womb is! I'll report you! Jean will suspend you again!"

"*Move* before I thump you down!"

They were out of control! Mrs. Harrison would have to put the beauties back inside their shells. In the face of hate and bullies she thanked God for 'Olive Oil Privilege'. She worked hard keeping a secret for it. Sex was legal but not for housekeeping managers to hand over back-shots to hotel guests from Trinidad that claimed to own oil down there. Worse when the back-shots should be reserved exclusively for the husbands!

Knowledge of the back-shot worked in Betsy's favor. It worked for Fay too. Mr. Harrison would not be happy if enlightened to it. Fortunately, Fay minded her own business unless someone interfered with her. She never told a secret except to the holder's face. She was plain and blunt. It was her culture. She was too direct to pussy foot around facts.

Everyone but Fay believed the manager was Betsy's friend by choice. It worked in Betsy's favor. Fay was a problem. She had too much popularity. Her charisma threatened to overshadow Betsy's shine! Even Jean liked her before she interfered with Fay's equilibrium to satisfy Betsy. It backfired by a secret back-shot revealed. Jean came out through the shredders.

Jean's biggest concern was a lingering question. Who told Fay? She could not question the subject. It was what it was. The back shot revealing led to the back shot puzzle and the back shot puzzle was depressing Jean Harrison at work.

After mulling over her threat to tell their manager, the girls backed down and walked away from Betsy. She took a sigh of relief and mulled over her own puzzle. What was it with room B 17? There was ever something exciting coming from that energy. With the ultimate experience of meeting Benny Benson, she hoped something exciting would come for her inside there too.

People were ashamed to give away back shots in fancy rooms these days – And in 2010 at that! She never received one. Something had to give for her at some point in life!

She did not fancy a head wrapping Trinidadian conman dressed up in skirt and claiming to be the 'oil sheik'. She had Benny to think about. If he tried the back shot on her she would go for a baby too! She would mother the next sprinter like Bolt. But, that wife of his was in there!

Some women got it all and took it for granted! When privileged folks got privileges they turned around to be ungrateful. Fay, the damned Jamaican, said that *'corn will not grow for the person with teeth to eat corn'*. Betsy was fit as a fiddle! She could do the split and bend and touch her toes. None of those ladies had *teeth to eat corn like she did*. Corn did not bear for her!

2

Betsy rested her left ear against room B 17 door. The Bensons were inside. They did not come out to get breakfast that morning!

Yesterday they went to dine around lunchtime. She cleaned their room without getting in their way. Most importantly, she did not want them to get in her way while she was cleaning and paying attention to details.

They would repeat the same routine as yesterday. Decent men like Benny knew nothing about vulgarity. Betsy distrusted the gold digger in his bed, who cheated her of a fair opportunity.

Some people pretended to be upright but if you listened to them in their bedrooms you would find out who they were. Last Christmas Eve she heard Apostle Elena James and her husband in that very room. What profanity! She told the girls about the fake woman of God. Fay said that respectable people were only lewd in the smutty minds of worthless and envious eavesdroppers! She did not even know what that meant. It sounded like an insult. That fool sided with the wrong doing preacher woman! When did God say eavesdropping was a sin?

Fay's comment was a load of crap! Decency was decency, even if you were having sex! Women of God should learn to curve their words and be holy vessels in all circumstances. How could she be God's vessel when she was telling her husband to drive that big cock? Was she driving out Jesus? Having sex was no right to be vulgar! Neither was it absolved because she thought no one else could hear her!

Fay claimed that Betsy spoke out of envy for every woman who sat on a penis. Betsy declared this the biggest lie in the history of lies! When had she ever envied a woman over a penis? Betsy Frazier had no time for people's business!

Right then she could bet that Benson bitch was inside the room being uncouth with the poor boy! She poked her ear against the door harder. There was no sound. Then she upped her level of concentration. That raucous woman's panting became audible. Mrs. Benson was moaning and saying that disgusting *'oh-oh-oh'* thing like a damned porn star! She kept calling his name as if he was not right there on top of her! *Disgusting bitch*!

Rochelle was no good for Benny Benson! What would she teach his children? *Oh-Oh-Oh* like little oh's? Why did Benny get married so soon? He was the most misled celebrity in history! Betsy knew that she could give him a better life. She was only forty two and her eggs were ticking. She waited for him. Now he was twenty three and Jezebel grabbed him!

When Betsy heard the woman's voice intensify she almost choked with rage! She felt like tearing off the 'no disturb' sign and barging in! The infidel was taking the lords name in vain screaming *"Oh Benny, oh God!"*

Rochelle was disrespectful to all things divine! How could she call God's name with pornography? The wiry woman agitated beneath her breath, *"Oh Benny, oh God* my butt? *Bitch*, you're going to hell!"

She drew away from the door in disgust and paced around inside the passageway. Betsy was boosted by an impatient rage that urged her to find recourse to justice *yesterday*! Justice for the trauma from Rochelle! How could she dare expose the world to her indecency!

Betsy went to listen again. The woman yelled so loud, it echoed and vibrated through the door. "Benny Benson! Don't stop or I'll kill you!"

"Damned bully, threatening that poor man!" Betsy declared in a whisper of rage. "Utter lack of decency! Low class bitch!"

This time Benny responded to his wife. "Sorry honey I'm coming!"

"You *crashed*?"

"Yes darling! I messed up this time!"

"It's ok! I made it!"

Betsy tore her eyes open with disappointed horror and mumbled in a hush, "*Sodom and Gomorra*! Jesus Christ Benny honey! Stop picking up on indecent leads! It's below you!"

They were silent now. Were they about to come out? Betsy stepped across the floor again. With her heart pounding hard against her ribcage, she put her ear to the door a second time. What if they suddenly pulled it open and caught her eavesdropping?

They were still in bed. She imagined them sprawled naked and their body parts entangling. It was revolting!

Betsy concentrated hard again. They were gasping for air. It sounded like Rochelle was suffocating to death. Betsy wished that so would be it! Something was breathtakingly good to her! Benny was selling cheap!

He lamented "Honey, the damned condom broke!"

"That's not my problem!" the wife reiterated, "I don't care if I'm knocked up? You're the one who's concerned about waiting until next year to breed!"

"I just wanted to..."

"We're married and you're rotten rich! We can afford children! What are we waiting for?"

He paused. Betsy bit her lips anxiously while awaiting his response. She wished he would put her in her place! That woman was not his type! Why should she have his children? Betsy would make a better mother!

Finally, he spoke, "I want children with you Rochelle. But we're so young. I don't want to rush into it."

"Well pardon me! We were best friends from the first grade in high school and we waited. We went to college together and we waited. Twelve years later you think I'm rushing into it! I'm infinitely confused!"

"Alright babes," he relented, "Scrap waiting! I'll be ready in a minute. No condoms this time!"

Rochelle giggled gleefully, Betsy winced disgustedly and a minute came in five seconds.

For the umpteenth time, the housekeeper cursed beneath her breath. They had nothing better to do! Clair-Castle Resort offered great entertainment! They wanted to spend all day trying to breed! Betsy gave up her rest day to work B 17 but there was porn going on inside! She had to live out the ordeal!

This time he humped so long that it was hard to believe. Betsy's ears told her that Rochelle was tremendously delighted! Not good at all!

Foolish people thought that this raucous nymphomaniac woman deserved that decent boy! Idiots claimed that she supported him with everything after his career ended with that injury before the Olympics. Crap! The entire island always supported Benny! Rochelle was a fraud!

Now and again traffic passed by and the wiry woman pretended to be waiting on someone. Some smiled at Betsy and looked knowingly at the no disturb sign. Some singles casted wishful eyes to the B 17 door. Betsy hated smart asses that seemed to guess what was going on! She could not unglue herself from Benny Benson's personal affair even to save face! Even if she was guilty of eavesdropping she was definitely not guilty for the ungodly deeds that took place inside. Fay was an idiot!

This time when it ended they were talking about going to get lunch. By now it was 12:25 PM. While they freshened up she strolled down the passage to a hundred feet from the door.

They came out glued onto each other and Betsy pretended like she just came. Benny wore white Bermuda shorts with Polo shirt and cap to match. She was dressed likewise but Betsy did not like looking at her! There was all that fuss on the news about her Coca Cola bottle shape and that she was beautiful! Betsy begged to differ! She was entitled to her own opinion!

She approached them, stepping hot like that Jennifer Lopez-looking Cassandra. She flung her head across her shoulder to see if her butt was protruding enough. She had to admit that, technically, it was not. That fucking Rochelle was watching her like a lesbian! Butt was not the only part of a woman's beauty! Just because she had a round firm butt like a South African did not make her better!

Rochelle saw her uniform and turned the no disturb sign. Benny guided Rochelle in Betsy's direction. Rochelle smiled at her. Betsy pretended not to notice, especially since that bitch stepped better than Cassandra. As they passed by, she offered in a friendly tone "Good afternoon Mr. Benson!"

Benny nodded half-heartedly but Rochelle looked at Betsy's name tag and said "Good morning Betsy! It's a beautiful morning isn't it?"

Betsy ignored her pleasantries! That Rochelle was an overly happy woman in this wretched life! Why was she taunting her? It was an afternoon! Because she got humped she believed the morning was beautiful! Smutty minded slut! She came acting like a princess. Betsy knew about her whorish behavior! She was corrupting him!

When they were out of sight, she fumbled for the key to unlock Heaven's gate. Betsy stepped inside the room and viewed the periphery. On day one, Rochelle's screaming got on her nerve. She took a break to give them time. When she returned they had left the room. She did not get to meet him then.

She stuck it out and met him today. Because of the goddamned wife, he did not even offer her a handshake! The tip would be on the bed as usual. She could use the extra cash but she was not on this job for the money. She had to be close to her only love!

She finished scanning the damage and shook her head. "You would think there was no woman in here!" she hissed with emphasized incredulity. "He has a very lazy wife! And she is nasty too!"

She went to gather the covers from the bed and off the floor. Something drew her attention. Betsy stopped to check the bin that they pulled next to their bedside. It was half empty as half the trash was beside and not inside it. What interested her most were not the pieces of tissue strewn across the floor. It was a balloon-like object resting beside the bin.

Sure enough, it was what she thought! It was a condom and a broken one at that!

Betsy remembered him telling her that the condom broke. She found that broken piece! It was leaking onto the floor but it still had a heavy load inside it. She hissed disgustedly but felt a hint of admiration at the same time. Benny was her favorite honk! He ejaculated like an elephant! Good for him. It was dangerous too. He would knock Rochelle up too soon! Betsy wished God would turn 'the wife' into a mule, if it was not too late!

She scooped up the condom with her bare hand, forgetting that she came with a hundred pairs of gloves. "Let me dispose of it," she stressed. "That woman is no good for the country!"

....

Fay Ambrose was clocking out. Jennifer and Cassandra walked into the room.

Of late, Fay worked on the West Side every day. It earned her more than everyone except Betsy. Betsy worked East Block with them but she was scheduled to capitalize on the most lucrative rooms on the day. They hated her! No one minded Fay's good fortune. She was tough and likable at the same time, even though her toughness came with a peculiar addiction to giggling.

"Hi Fay," the slightly stout, curvy beauty greeted the Jamaican, showing signs of reservation. Her slimmer friend waved in a bashful way. Fay eyed them suspiciously. "Hi yourselves!"

She was walking away. Cassandra pushed Jennifer in the back, propelling her into Fay. Fay giggled and stopped. "What is it?"

She asked the question but then remembered something and spoke again before they could respond. "Guess who I saw taking the yellow tour bus today!"

"Benny Benson!" the girls replied unanimously.

"Right! I didn't know he was here. I met his crazy sexy wife too. We spoke for ten minutes. They're *nice*!"

"Well, he's a nice guy. We expected that he would find a nice girl too," Cassandra surmised.

Fay nodded in agreement and would leave. Jennifer used her right hand to block her, "*Wait!*"

"*What?*"

"We want to talk to you about that very person!" Cassandra chipped in to support Jennifer.

"*Why*?"

"We want to know what Betsy Frazier is doing in there all day. We are scared to go and check. Mrs. Harrison threatened to fire anyone who goes into that aisle unless they are scheduled to work a room!"

"Don't look at me! It's not my job to watch other workers! Betsy's the eavesdropper not me! Jean Harrison knows I'm not lying too!" she giggled.

"We know that," Cassandra agreed, "We are way too curious about this one!"

Fay giggled. Betsy Frazier was sick! "Why me?"

"Like you had to ask!" Jennifer interjected, "Mrs. Harrison won't question you! She's afraid of you Fay!"

Fay giggled again. "You know what? I'll go because I'm getting curious too!"

Fay was unpredictable. She could go from hot to cold in a second. The girls eyeballed her questioningly. "I said I am going," she asserted with a giggle. She did not sound convincing.

Even when she giggled, no one was as sober as Fay. Yet they could never tell when to take her seriously.

"What's so funny?" Jennifer asked suspiciously.

"You two looking at me like hungry puppies!"

"It's because you're not moving!" Cassandra shot back, pushing her to the door, "*Go!*"

As she went, Jennifer opined, "She has a problem with giggling all day!"

"I know! I love it! She never worries about a thing!"

"I wish I was like her!"

"I wish you were too! I'm sick of comforting you!"

Fay arrived at B 17 and tested the lock on the door. It was open. She turned it gently and slipped inside the room. It was spotless. There were no issues at all. Betsy did the job well. It seemed she already left. As Fay turned to go, a thought struck her. She froze. Why did Betsy leave the door unlocked? Her lips transformed into a wry grin. The Jamaican turned back.

She turned on the camera on her Galaxy phone and stifled a giggle.

Fay went to the bathroom door, pulled it open suddenly and pointed the camera. There she was screaming in shock! Fay screamed too! But, as she was *Fay*, she composed herself instantly and hollered in the face of horror, "*You bombo-claat Abomination! Come out gal!*"

Betsy pulled out the flag and sprang to her feet.

"What are you doing woman? That's disgraceful! Your vagina will hate you!" Fay screamed disgustedly.

"*No!*" Betsy retorted in nervous defiance, even with the embarrassment. "Don't tell Cassandra and Jennifer lies on me! I treat my vagina better than you do yours!"

"You're abominable! I'm fucking traumatized!"

"A decent person is only lewd in the mind of a worthless and envious eavesdropper!" Betsy declared, using Fay's own philosophy against her.

Fay was stomped. She watched Betsy with open mouthed awe. Then Betsy pushed her luck and pushed her, "Get out! You shouldn't be here!"

Fay's rage boiled! The shredder came out! She slapped Betsy in the back of her neck and slapped her again to punctuate each sentence! *"Damned old fucking maid!"* SLAP!

"Abomination to womanhood!" SLAP!

"Abomination to Clair-Castle Hotel!" SLAP!

"Abomination to the sovereign flag of West Keyes!" SLAP!

"Stop behaving like a worthless girl!" SLAP!

"Behave like a forty year old raas woman!" SLAP!

"Leave out of Young Girls bombo-claat Alley!" SLAP!

"Stay in old woman's lane!" SLAP

"Look how the flag pole long!" SLAP!

"You give me goose pimples!" SLAP!

"You give me trauma!" SLAP!

"Lord I can't stop beating you!" SLAP!

"I will slap you till you bombo-claat dead! SLAP!

"No-no-no-no-no!" Betsy screamed in panic. "I'm dying! Don't hit me anymore! I'm ready to talk!"

....

Cassandra and Jennifer waited. Betsy came tailing Fay and eyeing her with suspicious apprehension. Her presence was restricting Fay! Something untoward *did* happen in B 17! Impossibly, it seemed Betsy had Fay's ticket! They did not expect to hear the report that day. Not with a mute Fay inside the room. Fay flashed them a guilty eye but shook her head to say that all was well. They were not buying it!

The Jamaican did not drive to work but now she had a car Key. Jennifer took notice. Fay gathered her stuff, nodded to the girls and went without a word.

The friends left defeated. Their gut feelings could not be wrong! They needed something to hold against Betsy Frazier! They were in the car park when Jennifer exclaimed suddenly, "Why does Fay have Betsy's car Key? They don't even like each other!"

"Maybe they do now! Something is *offish* here! She turned Fay into her *bitch* or something!"

"But Fay is no lesbian!"

"Neither was Mrs. Harrison."

Jennifer giggled unconvincingly, "*Jesus*! Betsy owns us all and she doesn't have balls! If Fay can break then life in this place is a hell hole!"

"My sentiments exactly!"

"At some point, night turns to day! We shall see what we shall see."

Just a stone's throw from where they were, Fay sat inside of Betsy's car. It was what it was. She was not letting down the girls. This one had nothing to do with them! It was her time to capitalize.

Today was not the day to judge Betsy. Fay did what was prudent at the time. She wished she could help Cassandra and Jennifer's cause. She had to help herself first! Betsy's judgment would come on a day of hallelujah. Someone would catch her with her panties down to her angles while she was bending over. They would catch her where *she* caught Jean Harrison! A puss and a dog had different luck!

Jean was still puzzling on how she knew what happened. The same man who bended her over told Fay just for laughs! He was as disgusting as Jean!

....

One week later, they were at the National Stadium. Cassandra brought a huge West Keyes flag for the cheering section. Jennifer had a medium sized one but Fay came empty handed. The girls guessed that she was being neutral. Her home country sent athletes to West Keyes for friendly contest. It would expose West Keyes upcoming athletes to superior competition. It was a high school/junior program.

The Jamaicans were on top of the world. High profile runners from high school level upwards were present.

"God knows I wish they brought Usain Bolt live!" Jennifer declared, waving at the field, although the races had not started yet.

"Maybe it would be a challenge for him to come when he's concentrating on his season," Fay opined.

"Maybe they didn't even try to get him here!" Jennifer chipped. She started waving again. Fay eyed the flag disgustedly. It was strange! Jennifer challenged, "So now you want to cheer for Jamaica! *What*? You're giving my flag 'the eye'? Here it is! In your face!" Jennifer shoved the flag at her.

Fay sprang to her feet hyperventilating. She flashed her hands like a child being spanked and screamed "No! The flag stick is too long! The flag stick is too long!"

Cassandra turned to her bewildered. This was the great Fay who never panicked! Why was she afraid of a flag? Jennifer pulled it away confused. "What did I do?"

Fay sobered up and caught her breath. "I'm ok! That was unexpected! Raise your flag – I'm good!"

Cassandra watched skeptically and surmised, "You panicked! It's like you had a 'flashback' of sorts. What up Fay? What're you not telling us?"

"Whatever happened is gone." Fay replied with finality, "If I tell you it won't be today!"

"Why are you *'flagophic'*? Do you hate our country?"

"No Jennifer!"

"Did they rape you with a flag?" Cassandra chipped in. "Girl tell your friends! We have your back!"

"No way!"

"So how did they rape you? On top of a flag?" Jennifer butted in.

"No one raped me girls. Come on!"

Cassandra closed one eye, scrutinizing her like a scientist. "People can get raped in more than one ways. If you don't tell us we can't help you."

Fay giggled, "I know but don't help!"

Jennifer chipped in again, "She's giggling Cass. She's fine! Maybe she had a temporary malfunction."

"This woman is hiding something Jennifer! And a flag is involved in it! Besides, Fay giggles for life or death!"

That day, Fay did not tell but she was stuck with the nickname *'Flagophobic'* or *'Flago'* for shorts.

3

Eight years later…

He tried everything with him but had no success! He was his flesh and blood but he could not run. It was frustrating! He even set the dog to chase him, for young Benny hated Casper drooling on him. Benjamin Benson JR could not run to save his life! The humongous Kangol caught up with him, knocked him to the ground and licked his face.

How did one of the fastest men in the world father a son who was the slowest? Capricia's daughter was two years younger. She could beat Benny with little effort!

Rochelle interrupted his thoughts, "Benny, look!"

She pointed to the other side of the field. A boy their son's age was practicing to run. Benny's eyes trailed across the pitch. His jaws dropped! No little boy could be that fast!

"Holy fuckolony!" he gasped. "If only our Benny would run like him! Imagine what I would do with that boy if he was my son!"

"I agree! That boy is awesome - Isn't he?"

"He is! Let's go make friends! I have to know him!"

Amazingly, the boy was training and motivating himself. Benny saw that passion and it seemed like a reflection of his past. The boy kept setting his own speed challenges. Benny used to do the same thing!

At first it seemed like the kid was by himself. Rochelle frowned, "Honey, why is he unsupervised?"

"I'm wondering the same thing!"

Then they noticed a car parked at the entrance to the playing field. The boy stopped practicing and sped to it, mimicking the sound of a race car.

"It seems like he's leaving," Benny said disappointed. The boy entered inside the vehicle.

"Unfortunate," she suggested, "But if he practices here, you might catch him on some other day."

"I hope so. Benny could train with him to get faster!"

The car moved off but it did not go through the exit. It drove alongside the pitch heading in their direction. Maybe there was a chance to meet him after all!

The car parked fifty feet from where they stood. The headlights blinked as if to send them a message. A short man in a black suit exited the vehicle from the driver's side. He was stocky, with an extra-large stomach. He carried a long black umbrella and appeared like the perfect replica of Penguin.

A long wiry leg pushed out from the back seat. A woman in a very lengthy dress that looked like leopard skin stepped out and pulled the boy with her. She looked exactly like Popeye's Olive Oil! What was going on with these characters?

"Penguin and Olive Oil!" Rochelle mused muffing a snicker. Benny reprimanded, "Behave yourself honey!"

She half-giggled before muffing it out. *"Sorry!"*

The trio walked ceremoniously to them. Rochelle frowned, "You think they're coming for your autograph when we should be getting theirs?"

"I don't know," Benny replied confused and stifling a laugh. "Somehow, it doesn't seem like it."

At ten feet away the man pointed his umbrella to Benny, "Good day Mr. Benson. My *intelligence* said that I would catch you here."

"Good day Mr...?"

"Sobers - Milton Sobers, Attorney at Law!"

Benny eyed his wife reflecting suspicion. Then he turned to address the attorney. "Well, Mr. 'Attorney at Law, Milton Sobers', why does your *intelligence* want you to catch me here?"

"Good question!" the lawyer wise-cracked. He swept his umbrella to his cohorts. "This, as you should know, is Miss Betsy Frazier. The boy beside her is her son Bentley Benson who is also yours as you would know!"

Benny turned to Rochelle for support. She was staring at the boy flabbergasted, oblivious to all else! She locked her eyes on him the moment they came within the ten-foot range! She did not need Sobers to pass the verdict! Not even identical twins could be more identical than that boy and her Benny Jnr!

She did not even hear what the attorney said. What she *saw* broke her heart instantly. *"The pig I fucking married!"* she hissed beneath her breath. Benny did not hear what she said. He assumed that she was venting disgust in his support.

Benny elbow-poked her for camaraderie. She eyed him with venom. He decided to deal with the absurdity on his own.

"This is ludicrous! I am the only athlete in the world who has only slept with one woman in his life! Go scam somewhere else! *Penguin!*"

Sobers shook his head and rolled his eyes in incredulity. "Do you see the boy son?"

"I'm *not* your son – And he is *not* mine!"

"Yes Benny," Rochelle interjected to emphasize Sober's question. "Do you see the fast-like-Benny-Benson and look-like-Benny-Benson boy you wanted to meet? *Abracadabra*! You have the boy you wanted!"

Benny ignored her and addressed the Penguin figure. "How does looking at a boy change the facts?"

"I am ashamed of you!" the attorney declared, "We called you the pride of West Keyes Island! Who could know you would become a dead beat dad? Would your idol Usain Bolt behave as you do?"

"He would too! No one wants an impostor Olive Oil baby mama, an impostor Penguin attorney, and an impostor son!"

Rochelle made like she was throwing up. "*Ugh!*" she announced, "I'm *sick* to the stomach!"

"What good man does not own up to his child?" Milton Sobers questioned. "Surely not Mr. Bolt! You are a wealthy man and your son is almost starving!"

"*Ugh! Ugh!*" Rochelle interjected.

"I don't know these people!" Benny reiterated.

"You would not know the boy. You did not care to do so! There is no way you do not know Miss Frazier. That would be impossible!"

"*You're* impossible!"

"Hah?" Rochelle questioned in amazement, widening her eyes at her once beloved Benny. "On the topic of *'who's impossible'*!"

Sobers glanced at Rochelle and thought he knew the problem. He changed his approach, stepped close to Benny and offered discretely, "Mr. Benson. Let's meet somewhere - You and me without the presence of Mrs. Benson. Would that jog your memory somewhat?"

Benny was adamant! He would never omit his wife from a thing in his life! Since they met in high school, he was the epitome of transparency. He vowed to keep it that way. He was the only faithful celebrity!

"Rochelle meets where I meet, *Mr. Penguin*! Get out of my face and go before I hit you!"

Sobers looked at the muscles on the big man and stepped back.

"Threats and violence will not help you with this. You should at least consider a DNA test, Mr. Benson. I'm going, but it's not over yet!"

Rochelle spun around in a rage and went to the car. She slammed the expensive AMG Mercedes door hard enough for him to know that she wanted to fuck it up! Sobers heard the door slam, turned around and winced. He could not help giving Benny the pitiful eye. A woman's wrath could hold no mercy!

Mrs. Benson sat and rocked hard to bear the fury. She saw the boys draw together with curiosity to question their reflections in each other.

Benny yelled at the messenger, "I'm going too! It is over! Unless you want to go through the shredder!" He held up his big fists to emphasize how the shredding would take place.

Rochelle hated what was transpiring. She heard Benny threaten to pulverize a helpless man to protect an impossible lie! She was no fool! She expected unfaithfulness from a celebrity. She was prepared to deal with it. Benny made it unforgiveable!

If he would only accept, apologize and beg her to forgive him, she would have a platform on which to start the atonement! He played like he was the victim instead of *her*! She was the one who lost *something*, especially with a Benny Benson tattoo on her! These things should be for life! No man liked to see another man's logo on his property! All his tattoos were about athletics! Athletics was paying him even in retirement! His tattoo was about to fail her!

Benny gave Sobers the middle finger. Rochelle watched with open mouth awe. He went to the kids, scooped up Olive Oil's boy and hurried to his car declaring "Let's go son. We're getting away from those devils and that bastard! *Now!*"

The boy was struggling and shouting "Put me down, sir! Put me down!" but yet he did not realize.

Benny pulled the back door and shoved the boy inside, beside the big dog. The Kangol bared its deadly fangs giving the boy an ultimatum to get out soon! He closed the door. The wiry woman screamed hysterically, "Kidnapper! Let my son go!"

He looked at the boy that was outside and then at the one inside his car. He took the *'other'* kid! It was certified by the dirty old green shirt he had on and the fact that Kangol did not know him! Rochelle watched distastefully. Benny was becoming irredeemable!

"Oops!" Benny offered with shame-faced apology. He saw the expression on the witnesses and lied to negate the question that dangled in the air. "It's because I didn't look at his face first!"

"You just called our son a bastard!" Rochelle stated matter-of-factually, pointing to Benjamin whom he left among the strangers. Benjamin was nervous and confused, thinking that his dad was swapping him.

Benny pulled the door, allowing the *stranger* to get out. Bentley ran to his mother for freedom. Rochelle asked Benny sarcastically, "He's not yours - Is he?"

Benny shook his head disgustedly. "I only have one son!" he agitated. "Come on Benny! What the devil are you waiting for?"

The attorney cut in, "He's waiting for his father to introduce him to his brother!"

Rochelle added, "Maybe he's not sure if he's being swapped!"

Betsy threw in, "You know he's yours! That's why you tried to switch him with the bastard!"

Sobers waved his hand belatedly to cut off Betsy's ill advisable insult. It was too late! Rochelle flew out of the car to question, "Who's the bastard fiddle foot Olive Oil woman?"

"Damn you dirty wife! Jesus will curse you!"

The enraged wife kicked off her shoes and became frisky on her feet. Betsy backed away intimidated. Rochelle kept approaching her and she kept backing off. "Come here Betsy Frazier! *Pleeaasse* come here!" the woman pleaded, desperate to pacify her anger.

"No! I won't come!"

"*Oh*! I'm begging you *honey*! Come to my arms!"

Milton Sobers backed away from Benny, while backing the woman away from Rochelle. Seeing that Rochelle was completely ticked off and ready to go, he backed both clients into the old Toyota, took the wheels and sped off! "I'll be coming back to you Mr. Benson!" he promised. He turned to Betsy and advised, "No insolence next time, please!"

"I could not resist it! That's a foul mouthed woman who uses Jesus' name with pornography!"

"She was not insulting you."

"She's a bitch who took my man! She thinks she's all that because she's more beautiful than Cassandra!"

"Who's Cassandra?"

Benny watched the car pull away. He felt energized by what he saw as Rochelle's support. "Go away Penguin!" the celebrity bellowed, showing the middle finger again. "Go back to Goddamned City!"

"It's not *Goddamned City*!" Rochelle agitated, finding everything about Benny irritating! "It's Gotham City you piece of *shit*!"

"*Sorry honey*!" he said, not knowing what else to say.

"Super *fuck you*, Benny Benson! I'm not your honey! Close your ears, Benny Jnr!"

They went back inside the car. He pleaded, "I don't deserve this Rochelle!"

"I know but *I* deserve it! I'm too damned good for you Benny Benson! I'll tell you what you deserve! You deserve your feisty fiddle foot fifty-looking cradle robbing baby mother! I don't know how you managed a hard on for her!" She glanced over her shoulder, "Did you put on the headphones Benny Jnr. I said to close your ears!"

From the back seat Benjamin was still amused by Rochelle's fine sense of poetry. Benny turned to give him the *puckered eyes*. "Put on the damned headphones boy! And turn on the music! *Now!*"

"Leave my son alone you goddamned two-timing Olive humping dead beat dad!"

Benny rubbed his forehead, tearing at the skin in frustration, "Why would I lie to you, honey?"

"Because you're a cheating coward! Not even your biased mother will believe you Benny!"

"Crap! Mama will always support me!"

"We'll live to see! *Oh!* On the topic of who deserves what…" she paused to ensure that Benny Jnr. was not listening. Then she lowered her voice. "You think it's fair for me to be stuck with your tattoo for life?"

"A tattoo is just a tattoo Rochelle!"

"Your dirty name on my *pussy* – if I must leave you – Benny?" she hissed hysterically. Benny Jnr. whistled, clucked his tongue and lamented *"Nooo wayyy!"*

....

He took up Rochelle's challenge and called his mother to prove his point. The next day she came to spend a week consoling him.

Mother Benson hardly ever agreed with Rochelle on anything! By the time he finished explaining *the situation* to old Mother Benson, she was hunching up in a corner and whispering with Rochelle all the time! Now and again, one of them would peep to see that he was not in the hearing range. They were best friends now, like bench and bottom! She consoled Rochelle all day long, forgetting who called her!

He was the innocent victim. No one cared! Not even the woman who brought him into this world!

She came on Sunday evening. When he finished relating the story to her, she was asking skeptical questions. *"Why do you think you mistakenly took the wrong boy Benny"!*

"Why would the kids be shocked to see each other?"

"Benjamin's mother couldn't tell him apart Benny?"

"Are you sure you don't remember 'an incident'? No famous athlete is perfect!"

"Jesus, Mama! There were no *'incidents'*!"

"I understand. Your father was unfaithful once. He said that *'there were no incidents'*. Not saying *'like father like son'* but I suggest you talk to him about how you proceed from here."

When he asked if she believed him, she hummed, pretending like she did not hear the question. When he asked if she disbelieved, she said, *"I would not say so."*

She would break to go gossip with Rochelle. Her body language told how deep into Rochelle she was getting! Rochelle claimed that he shackled her vagina for life so it was fair to steal his mother!

They attacked him together! Rochelle demanded that he accept the truth and apologize. His mother reminded him that she did not say he was guilty before adding that an apology never killed anyone.

When he overheard Mother Benson telling Rochelle that she would find her grandson and bring him home, it was the final straw! Although Rochelle hated Betsy, she had empathy for the boy. "You have to help that child. As for me, I don't know what I will do yet."

The above meant she was threatening to leave him! She would leave her husband for being faithful! He never breached the rules of engagement concerning her tattoo! She blamed him for things he did not do! She was forcing him to be the father of someone else's child! No way would he apologize for jack shit!

At their next attack, he had to emphasize his truth. He would swear by God's name to impress his Christian mother. When he said, "Mama, may God punish me if I'm lying!" Mother Benson instinctively clutched at her heart. Rochelle swayed on her feet like she would faint. Benny Jnr. passed by, rolled his eyes and whistled!

He turned to the kid to reprimand him. Mother Benson intervened, "Leave the boy alone!"

Rochelle cackled with mocked sarcasm. The boy chuckled and left. Then the rain came, playing pit-a-pat on their luxurious window pane. Distant thunders rumbled. The boy returned and positioned at the door.

Benny had an idea! "If I am lying," he asserted, "May God's lightning strike and electrocute me!"

Rochelle shrieked impulsively. The boy half-whistled reflexively. Mother Benson half uttered unintentionally but fear of a mighty truth-loving god kept her mouth closed. She turned to see the boy eavesdropping and waved him away with a fan of her palm. Benny was satisfied with the effect of his truth utterance. He took the opportunity to add "And if I am lying, may the thunder roll and break my neck!"

Immediately there was an incredible peal of lightning. Thunder came simultaneously, shaking the foundation of the Benson mansion! Rochelle screamed. Mother Benson shouted an apology to God, taking responsibility as she was the mother.

Benny Benson was on his knees underneath the dining table shaking and wondering if God was in it too. The boy charged back to the room. He had both hands on top of his head, inquiring "Mama! Mama! Is Daddy dead yet?"

4

Betsy felt that it would work without a DNA test. She thought that pressure would break the pipe! Benny did not relent, even as Mother and Father Benson played grandparents to Bentley. It did not break the big athlete! He insisted that he was not the father and that they brought a stranger to their home.

Rochelle gave him an ultimatum. Apologize or face the consequences! She threatened that she would not walk out with only half of his riches. He would pay dearly for that tattoo! It was an unlikely threat but he hated the thought of it. She was his manager from day one. He focused on athletics and she controlled his investments. He had many endorsement deals but they were still coming unabated.

He had not to worry about losing too much. She worked, he paid her. He owed her nothing! This was not America. She could not claim in excess of what was reasonable. The most she could do was steal from him. That would be criminal! He could fire her and just play his part as a husband and provider. That he could not do if it killed him. He simply lived with her threats! He would just let her make her move.

He sent her to college so she could be his manager. She did well as a manager. Not as a business partner. She had her own career. Benny was a business tycoon on the island. He built an empire on his fame. He capitalized on the spending power of over four million people. Anywhere else in the world, his international status could not make him that big a star.

People who thought that prenuptials were unfair were dead wrong. As his adviser, Rochelle believed that it would be unfair to him to not have one! He was not a business genius but he felt like she was bluffing. Since she was not on his side, he needed a personal adviser.

In his country no other sprinter was world renowned. He won all his Olympic heats and made the finals before crashing out due to injury. He won international gold medals in both junior and senior championships. He was to West Keyes as Bolt was to Jamaica. West Keyes was a good place for business. Anyone with money and brains could become a mighty force in five years. Rochelle proved it with the Benny Benson legacy.

Rochelle was no gold digger! Her hysteria was about a tattoo! He never breached the tattoo agreement!

Benny took her family out of poverty. He bought her father his first car, which he was still driving. He built their house in the beautiful Hansel Folk Community. Rochelle was not ungrateful. She gave him value too! If he was guilty he would not blame her.

She was sentimental about her 'body parts'. He agreed that they were priceless but he was innocent. No one tattooed her vagina expecting to go back single! He asked her to do it! She said 'No' but he besieged her to put the shackle on it! That was the damage for which she demanded a humongous redress!

She loved him so that forgiving him would be easy! She would not forgive the unrepentant! He had too much pride in his lies! If the thunder took up his challenge that evening, young Benny would lose a father. It proved he was careless! Who would challenge God with lying lips? Repentance was all it took!

....

It took more than a week but they came. The pendulum swung in Benny's favor when the fathers arrived. Father Benson and Rochelle's father, Eric Darlin, met in Benny's office. It did not seem like an important meeting - just men hanging out and drinking shit loads of alcohol. Benny stored tons of expensive liquor in there. It was their favorite place in life.

The last family meeting they were so stoned, their words turned into slurs without syllables. No one could decipher them. It was about to happen again!

At the end of their unconventional formality, the intoxicated fathers came to the living room to pass the verdict. They came on dry land seeming to be swimming. Eric was the spokesman. First he called out Rochelle. "My daughter," he slurred, "what is the problem with you and your beautiful wife."

Instead of correcting his error she answered the question that he intended to ask, "He has an outside child with *Olive Oil* and he won't admit it!"

"Did you prove that child is his and not yours?" the masterful drunk asked with an intelligent air. "How do you know that the child has Olive Oil? What kind of disease is that anyway? Did he catch it because he was outside? Why didn't you bring him inside?"

She looked at him with one eye and a frown, deciphering. "I saw the child! It's definitely his!"

"You saw it? That's why you are the guilty party and not Benny!"

"*What* Daddy?"

"Stop questioning your father's years of intelligence! Apologize to your husband for three reasons!" He marked off one on his finger, "One is that a DNA test does not constitute your eyes." he paused, blinked confusedly and said, "Turn number one around to top to bottom and make more sense." He blinked again, "Or just put the right constitution in the right place!"

He staggered forward struggling to steady himself. "The second is that, when he was on that woman, he was in a better position to know the truth. You were not there. You were not between the leg or the sheet. You must believe his word and not know it is a lie! For God said *'blessed are the believers to believe in a lie'*! For faith without works is dead. Work, believe and live!"

He paused. "And, I forgot the third one...You interrupted and took the words out of my mouth!"

Rochelle glanced around stupefied, "No one interrupted you Daddy."

He staggered forward again, concentrating hard to brace himself and regain his balance. "It was my walk that interrupted my talk!"

He was trying to recall something. Finally he asked Rochelle. "What did I just say my daughter?"

"You said that he's in a better position to know if he was on top of that woman. You said, even if he was between her legs under the sheet, I would not know. I was not there. Therefore I have no right to assume that what he says is a lie. I should give him the benefit of the doubt instead of presuming that he's lying."

"*Good girl*! *Shit* I didn't know what I was saying!"

Eric turned to Father Benson, who was as drunk as he was, "What was the third one old devil?" he asked, poking a finger at his colleague. Father Benson saw him rocking as if about to collapse and chuckled, "You're too fucking drunk to remember shit!"

"Remember two and I'll remember three Nathan Benson!" the thinner drunk countered, confusing everyone.

Father Benson laughed heartily at his friend's stupidity, "What the fuck is this guy saying? Remember three and I must remember two? Who is going to remember the third one?"

"You, Nathan!" Mother Benson replied impatiently.

"Why me?"

"Because you were in the doggone meeting with Eric telling him what to say!" Mrs. Darlin offered in support.

"Alright!" he conceded begrudgingly. "Since you claim that I said what I didn't! I told him about the third one. I didn't tell him about a flipping number three!"

"What is the third one, Nathan?"

"So," Nathan declared, rocking and counting his fingers to find it. "The third one is: Guilty until proven innocent! You don't win a case because you're right! You win because they believe you!"

"You win because you fucking prove the case, Nathan!" Eric snapped agitated. "It's your own words but you forget!"

"*Yes*...but please quit swearing in front of the *fucking* case," Father Benson reprimanded. Then he continued to lay out the judgment. "And if you prove the case, it's because a DNA proves the test...or some shit like that!"

"Right brother!" Eric applauded, "And if Benny's innocent tonight, then Rochelle is guilty until tomorrow…after the test proves he's in the shit! Rochelle apologizes tonight and Benny apologizes on the day the trial ends and the fan hits shit away! Innocent tonight and guilty tomorrow! That's the law!"

At that point, Nathan held up his hand to draw all attention, "Do you people understand?" he queried, "Anyone who doesn't get it, speak now or forever peace you withhold in a court of flaw!"

Their confusing tongues had spoken clearly. Rochelle was fuming, but not because she thought that the drunks were wrong. She was fuming without a cause; for she knew that she was technically as wrong as they said. She was going to have to apologize tonight! Tomorrow she would lead the charge to have that DNA test done and then ask Benny to apologize. As he would not, she would take it from there! At that point, she would justify her right to react as she pleased.

....

The chubby lawyer was impatient. "They are asking for a DNA test, which would exonerate you. You don't agree to it. What do you want then, Miss Betsy?"

"I want Benny to stand up to his responsibilities! His parents accept Bentley. Why can't he?"

"The court will demand a DNA test as well. Benny's parents accepted him on presumption only! That has nothing to do with the real case."

"What do you mean, Mr. Sobers? What's to presume? Do you have any doubts? I want my Benny to own me!"

"It's not about him owning *you* Miss Betsy. I'm not saying I doubt you but frankly, I cannot be sure either. People don't prove paternity by looking at the child!"

"Even when it's identical to its Papa?"

"Sure! I've seen near-identical strangers before. It's natural to doubt a woman who doesn't want to do the test. Did you sleep with him or are you lying? Benny Benson claims that you are pulling a trick because you discovered that your child looks like him."

"*Me*? And why would I do such a low down thing? He's lying!"

"Then take up his challenge and prove it. Even his mother and wife are supporting him now. No one believes you anymore! Agree to a DNA test and let's move on. If you expect this case to be based on the superficial, you do not need a lawyer. You agreed to the test before I took this case. You must deliver now!"

"*No*! It insults my integrity! Benny needs to accept and take care of his Bentley!"

"With all your sentiments, you must remember that his parents are not responsible for child support. Benny should be but he won't until you prove it beyond a shadow of a doubt! I can do so much and nothing more. If you do not agree to carry out what we agreed on, this case cannot proceed any further. I will bill you now and good luck, Miss Betsy Frazier."

"No way! This case is far from over! My Benny Benson will pay my legal fees!"

"He's *your* Benny Benson now, is he? I don't see him paying a dime! Especially after what you stirred up caused his wife to threaten to take more than half his estate!"

"Rochelle is taking more than half? Then what about mine? Can I have the other half?"

Mr. Sobers scratched his head and winced, seemingly fatigued. "You're going for child support. What on earth could qualify you for half of this man's estate?"

"I do have his son you know."

Sobers shook his head in disgust. "I'm leaving now, Miss Frazier! Your bill will come in the mail!"

She watched in shock as he left her. The attorney stopped at the door and said matter-of-factually, "You know, people are really beginning to doubt you."

"Why should they Mr. Sobers?" she questioned hoarsely.

"If you were telling the truth you would go for a DNA test *yesterday*! This is insane! I can't convince you, so goodbye!" He grabbed his umbrella and his 'Penguin's hat' and slipped through the door.

The chubby man went to his car and drove off down the street. As he went, his heart sank inside him. No two days were alike. He was happy and hopeful yesterday. Today his life was full of crap! He embarrassed himself with this mad woman! Why did he take a silly case? He wondered why he believed Betsy Frazier in the first place. Just days ago he was on track to be a hero. He was on TV, on the radio and all of West Keyes knew him. Now he was a loser...again.

She could not do the test! Benny was right! She hatched the plan thinking that people would buy into the fact that Bentley seemed identical to Benny. She was in for a rude awakening! So was he! He went to law school for a madwoman to turn him into a byword!

When he took the case, he decided not to charge her a fee until Benny paid over. He was confident of a big payday. All he had now was to try and recoup his cost. His option was to stay invisible for a while. The ridicule would be hard to bear! Sure, it would not bother Betsy too much. She was used to it! Plus, she was too mad to care!

Now Benny was suing them both for public mischief and defamation of character. He made a case that they were cohorts in a game of scamming. As long as Betsy failed to do the test he would have a good case too!

He turned on the radio. It was on every talk show. He felt the ridicule that Benny Benson had to undergo when he started putting pressure on him through the media. Now that Betsy opted out of the test, they were the ones facing the public rage. Instead of listening to them labeling Benny as a dead beat dad, he had to listen to them calling him a worthless crooked lawyer. He did not care what they called Betsy - and they were calling her many ungodly things. She deserved it all! She was the one who got him into it!

With all that was at stake, Betsy claimed she hated DNA tests as they made her feel like a whore.

5

He accepted her apology and they were like husband and wife again. At least they were to a reasonable degree. She would soon get used to believing the truth. Everything would be fine. The grandparents were used to having Bentley around. They loved him as their own. He reminded them of little Benny back in the days!

Rochelle gave up on pitching to Betsy to have the test done. She concentrated on making atonement to Benny. She was hard on him! It was wrong to threaten him and mention divorce. She went as far as to bring his estate into question, acting like a gold digger! She told him sorry a thousand times. He easily forgave her!

Then the telephone rang. Rochelle went to it and took the call. Milton Sobers was on the line! Betsy Frazier agreed to do the test after all. Instantly, she went back to the dark side!

That Sunday afternoon he wanted to cook *something special*. Benny was happy up to the moment she came and yelled, "Betsy Frasier will do the test tomorrow! I'll get you by the balls now, you piece of *shit*!"

As it hit the airwaves the pressure shifted again. Betsy was the innocent victim. Public opinion elevated Milton back to the position of noble attorney. Benny fell back to the pits of degradation. He was the infamous promiscuous and disingenuous deadbeat dad!

Milton Sobers took on new confidence. She agreeing to a test proved she was telling the truth! He had no doubt whatsoever. He could smell Benny Benson's hundred dollar notes. He would crush Benny hard!

Betsy labored for nine months to bring his child into the world. Then she struggled alone for another eight years! He had a lot to pay back for being deadbeat!

Out of four million people on the island, only Benny Benson and Betsy Frazier knew the truth. She had to know that the test would exonerate him and not her! Why did she agree to it? She was desperate! Rochelle put pressure on her! She made a futile decision to solve one problem at the cost of another. He was not sorry for her! Evil Betsy would faint after the judge read the test results! He was ready to laugh! Within hours, Rochelle's foolish attitude would change too.

Who was Betsy Frazier? Why was she doing this to him? He would not counter sue as planned. He wanted to forget the issue! He wanted his old life back *now*!

Betsy Frazier rocked in her favorite rocking chair watching the news. Her mind was elsewhere.

"Benny my love!" she crooned. "Look what you did to me! I'm shaming myself for you with a DNA test! Please accept your Bentley and then be mine!"

She watched the people lambast him. "Sorry Benny! I didn't mean to make them curse you! Tomorrow I might die of shame. That DNA test might kill me!"

....

Mother Benson set the table and sat for dinner with Nathan. Bentley was on their minds. The court would settle it finally! They would have him in their lives in spite of Benny. They hoped he would apologize to Rochelle. She refused to compromise her principle. No one could blame her.

Nathan chuckled and slurred, "I hope that Eric made it home on safety. He cannot drive and hold his liquor! He drank a keg and left pretending like he's sober! She's going to find out when his nonsense begins to talk and he'll not be unsober!"

Mrs. Benson eyed him with critical one eye poking suspicion and asked, "Are you drunk Nathan? You sound so!"

"You cannot tell a sound by the cover! You have to look inside the drunk! That's not fair to accuse him!"

She was thinking deeply, ignoring his defensive self righteous diatribe. "You know what, Nathan?"

"What is it?"

"I'm disappointed with Benny! Those boys even have the same birthdays! They were born one hour apart. Bentley is the older one!"

"So they're one and two twins, in a universal way?"

"Right! Bentley is so adorable!"

"I know, but adorable in one is in two. All men are born equal! Benny is laid back but his book is smart in his homework, like Rochelle. Bentley is running and buying cars and Hennessy like his disowning daddy! And then Eric will come and drink it all off like a big fucking gobble mouth fish!"

Mrs. Benson bit her lips to keep from laughing. Nathan and Eric were two of a kind! Unless they were drunk, you could not pick sense out of their nonsense!

She composed herself. "Benny Jnr. is his mother's child! Benny gave the wrong one his name!"

"Athletics is not the only star in the galaxy woman! If he stars in scholarship and goes to Mars, it's still a star!"

"That's true! But what if Rochelle carries out her threats?"

"It's not her fault! She gave him a choice on her vagina! He should pick the apology or leave the tattoo!"

"She threatens to bleed him dry!"

"Threatening Benny cannot do what the law cannot do! You watch too much TV in America! You did not put me on your vagina and I demand for disrespect!"

"If I did I wouldn't leave you over one outside child!" she confided. Then she giggled mischievously and asked, "What if I came with some other guy's tattoo?"

"Then I shall buy the sandpaper! It's good to scrub!"

She winced and hastily forgot his comment. "Well, that's what Benny has to pay for. Maybe it's better for her to stick with him."

"She should buy him the sandpaper instead of going into a nunnery!"

....

The Darlins sat on the veranda having a conversation. They knew what was coming the next day. Rochelle was right but what the heck? Apologies were overrated! For their sake, she should stay with Benny regardless! He made them happy! She was too mean and stuck up! Now she threatened to make them lose him! He gave them everything their hearts desired. But *she* – their own daughter, never once considered sparing a penny!

Mrs. Darlin shook her head distastefully. Eric slurred, "I know! No more bottles of Moet for me!"

He thought hard then frowned and said, "Babes."

"Yes Eric?"

"Does Benny have a bad heart?"

"Benny is a very loving person. Maybe he's naïve with this one. It's hard to imagine what that old woman experienced and what the child is going through without a caring dad."

"Betsy Frazier experienced nothing special!" he slurred, "It's not rocket of scientist! Babies have women every day!"

She paused and then frowned. "It's not common for a forty two year old ungreased Jezebel to push out a ten pound boy!" She eyed him suspiciously. "Are you drunk *Mr. Drunk*? How the hell did you drive us home?"

Eric winced then blinked stupidly and declared, "I don't say I'm drunk and not drunk but no comment."

He was agonizing about the 'ungreased' part. When he could not hold it any longer he opined, "Betsy Frazier is not forty three Babes. She's fifty one! Forty three could find grease but fifty one is dry Sahara!"

"What is that gibberish, Drunkie? Betsy had the child eight years ago! She was only forty three then!"

"*Shit*! I forgot to count from time before to the end!"

"*Shit* I love you but you drink too much!"

....

Fay sat inside her new car. She traded in the one she received from Betsy years before. She was watching the hearing on her Galaxy s6.

"Raas! This is crazy!" she marveled. Nine years ago, Betsy got pregnant as an old fowl. No one knew the boy's father! It was certainly not Benny Benson, for she knew he did not touch her! She did not care who the child looked like! What was Betsy up to this time?

The staff at West Keyes Hotel knew her as coo-coo. This episode beat all the rest! Yes, she was obsessed with the poor fellow. Bringing him a child that she knew was not his was passed insanity!

That Monday morning a timid Betsy walked into the courtroom. Milton Sobers coaxed her on. He brought her to the front of the room and ushered her to her seat. Benny Benson had not turned up yet. Rochelle was there seeming quite impatient.

The media televised the spectacle for the benefit of the citizens of West Keyes Island. A vast number of people gathered, having to stand and wait outside. Those that could not turn up at the courthouse in the capital drew close to their television screens. Others kept their radios close to their ears. Ninety-nine percent of citizens felt that the child was his. They wished he would come good and stand up as a role model.

Mr. Sobers looked at his watch. It was 9:59 AM. No sign of the defendant yet! He peeked around Betsy's body to see those gathered in his corner. His attorney Barnaby was there. Would Benjamin Benson be late for court? As soon as the thought struck, Judge Maria Mason arrived. Immediately, Benny made his entrance!

The celebrity was determined to make a show of confidence. His happy face was on! It was his day of jubilee. He spent hard cash for the occasion. It was worth the trouble to him. He stared at Betsy as he went by. She saw him and looked away ashamed.

Rochelle saw him coming to her. She went to the back seat. He ignored her behavior. It was his day. She would see how wrong she was!

He sat beside Attorney Barnaby. The court was called to order. Judge Mason wasted no time. She wanted to get it over with and let the lawyers worry about the result. She would have Benny in court again soon! He would not get away like her dead beat dad!

Benny Benson was too much of a case all by himself. She heard about *the tattoo*! That ticked her off most! How dared these wealthy men! They made a trend out of demanding tattoos from women! Then they would screw up the relationships!

One Commissioner of Police left a young female lawyer stuck with his tattoo! The devil now lived in the South of France! Fifteen years later she still had to answer the damning question, "*Whose tattoo that*?"

Maria Mason knew that the sight of one tattoo could make a man instantly impotent! By the time they were done querying its origin, it was over! She could seriously relate to poor Rochelle Benson!

Today was not about the tattoo! It was about the DNA test result she would read! She knew what it had to be! She felt for that poor old-*ish* woman! She was all of forty one when he was twenty-three but he still used her! Thirteen years his senior! He should be ashamed!

She felt for poor Rochelle Benson. She saw her walk away when he came near her. Rochelle kept muttering underneath her breath and Maria beckoned to her. "Mrs. Benson, I see that you have much on your mind. How are you feeling right now?"

Rochelle made to speak. Maria stopped and beckoned her forward. "Please come right up, and get that off your chest!"

As she was not one for the limelight Benny expected her to pass on the offer. Instead Rochelle declared "Thanks Your Honor!" and went with emphazised zeal.

"Say what you have on your mind!"

Rochelle eyed her husband spitefully and said, "I was betrayed Your Honor! Benny Benson took my innocence! I was a virgin before I met him! He was a virgin too but I never violated the sanctity of this relationship. I cannot be pure for anyone else at this point! These tattoos complicate the issue too! That child is not the only one who needs justice!"

Before the judge could respond, Betsy shouted to Benny "Baby I'm still a virgin!"

The entire court broke out in raucous uncontainable laughter. Maria Mason's jaws dropped. She took off her classes and wiped them again. Then she refitted them and scrutinized Betsy. *"How*? Explain *that* trick to me."

At that, the audience intensified the sound of hilarity. Maria let them laugh until they were done. This was too much! When it quieted down she strummed her fingers waiting on Betsy to explain. Her stubby lawyer pushed up his hand like a kindergarten child.

"Yes Mr. Sobers! Are you *explaining* it for her? Let's hear from you! This will be *interesting*!"

"She's talking *figuratively* Your Honor! That has to be obvious! I don't know why everyone took it literally!"

"It is because we are literally dealing with a court case!" Mario offered matter of factually.

So...in all the tension, she had them stand before her. She opened the envelope. "In the case of Mr. Benjamin Bentley Benson and Betsy Frazier, we have the test results. It states clearly, with ninety-nine-point nine percent certainty, that Benjamin Benson is the boy's father! We shall have another day in court! We will take a recess and then I'll let you all know that date!"

Benny made a muffled shriek. The wiry Attorney Barnaby reached out to break his fall. His massive bodyweight blew Billy Barnaby's hand away like paper. The athlete crashed on his back with a huge thud.

"What's his problem?" the judge queried annoyed.

"My client fainted, Your Honor!"

"*Fainted*? Why would he be shocked? He's still pretending! Get this dead beat dad out of here!"

"Dead beat husband too!" Rochelle whispered matter-of-factually locking eyes with the judge. Rochelle knew he fainted. She had no heart to care!

Betsy hustled to Benny. Sobers tried to stop her. She shoved him off screaming, "Benny my love! I didn't mean to hurt you! She doesn't love you but I do!"

Rochelle watched her with revulsion. "He's all yours!"

"You're so kind Rochelle! *Thank you!*"

Benny heard Betsy's voice. It shocked him to recovery. He found that he was in her arms and fainted again!

"My darling!" Betsy cooed, "Oh my darling!"

Barnaby shoved her off, "Get away! Don't you see you're killing him?"

Cathie Crew was in her living room watching the case on TV. "*Crap!*" she declared.

Most people embraced the superficial, disregarding the inner truths. When people spoke at the spur of the moment they usually spoke truth. She had a crush on Benny for as long as she was old enough to admit it! Maybe it clouded her mind but she did not care!

Benny was not insane but he said things that made him seem insane. Was it a case where the truth was the anomaly? Why did Betsy declare that she was a virgin at the spur of that moment to compete with Rochelle?

She would take Betsy's words seriously! The fact that she claimed the impossible only equated Benny's impossible words. Everyone was judging him! Their judgments were predetermined and one-sided!

....

Benny managed to rise and exit the building. He tried avoiding the media. As he hit the pavement they creamed him! He kept repeating, "I swear I didn't do it!" and "She framed me!"

"What do you mean she framed you?"

"You heard what she said! She's still a virgin! I didn't touch her! No sane person would touch her!"

Those statements did not help. He did not care! He would go down telling the truth! He thought about requesting another test at a different institution of his choice but changed his mind. He lost the will to fight!

Benny thought all would get back to normal that day. It got impossibly worse! Rochelle was his greatest worry but he did nothing to hurt her! He did not lie to get with her. He would not lie to keep her! He could not live a lie for life! He was real; whatever fate decreed.

No more was he desperate for Rochelle. He was angry at her! She would wait but an apology would not come! Let her make impossible threats! There were other business brains on the island! His new adviser was not only beautiful. She was sharp too!

Rochelle could not take half his estate without taking him along. Benjamin Bentley Benson was the entire brand. She could attain no right to own him! The people of West Keyes would cuss him today and love him tomorrow. This awful lie was the one blemish on his record. Business was not letting up.

Cathie said that Rochelle could not take anything that he did not give her! The record showed that she got her reasonable share in her salary. He stood up to his responsibilities as a husband. The court would insist that he gave her a justifiable one time separation payment. If he gave her a puny million and a house the court would agree that it was enough. Rochelle was good enough to make him a good prenuptial contract!

He would have to pay child support if she won custody. Since the court would rule that he was in the wrong, she would have the advantage. If he fired her before the hearing, he would regain the advantage.

Rochelle deserved more than handouts. He gladly agreed! He was Benny and not *her*! If she left him she would lose more than she could gain hands down.

Next day, the front page of the West Keyes's News said *"He said no sane person would touch her but she had his child! Benny Benson adds insult to infidelity!"*

....

Cathie Crew was a young corporate lawyer with little working experience under her belt. She did not want to be in the same room as Rochelle! That was weird. She was a professional and he was paying for services she rendered to him.

She wanted to think that it was side effects of being between him, her and his estate. That was untrue. Cathie's crush on Benny induced guilt! She felt he was telling the truth even with the evidence stacked against him. Now that he was proven the liar beyond a shadow of a doubt, she still had that ludicrous belief in Benny Benson's impossible truth. Cathie knew he chose her for believing in him. He had the best choices in the land. Her qualification was on paper.

She watched it play out in court until he fainted. He did not expect to be disproven! She alone noticed *that*!

She saw Betsy Frazier's interview. Betsy was in a permanent state of apology. She was guilty of *something*. She claimed she did not want to hurt him by going public with the case. Those words went much deeper to Cathie. They came across differently to the rest of West Keyes. They adored her for being 'nice'! They cussed Benny for hurting her! This woman made Cathie sick to the core!

Reporter: "So, Miss Frazier. Can you tell us how you met Benny?

Betsy: "Yes! I met my love nine years ago at the West Keyes' Clair-Castle Hotel where I work."

Reporter: "I see. So what were you? A waitress, room service attendant? What?"

Betsy: "He was in the honeymoon suite in Room B 17. I was the housekeeper who did his room."

Reporter: "You met Benny on his honeymoon and he slept with you? How? Where was his wife in all of this?"

Betsy: "She was with him all the time!"

Reporter: "She was? Just like Benny she claims not to know you!"

Betsy: "She's lying! We spoke!"

Reporter: "What did you speak about?"

Betsy: "She was telling me good morning and making conversation about the weather. I did not answer her because I was busy talking to my Benny."

Reporter: "Your Benny? And did his wife know that he was yours?"

Betsy: "Sorry, I can't say any more!"

Reporter: "Why can't you, Miss Frazier?"

Betsy: "It's complicated. You will not understand it!"

Reporter: "Try me, Miss Frazier!"

Betsy hustled off to her Lawyer who was looking for her. The reporter tailed her, "When did you get pregnant for Mr. Benson?"

"The day I met him!"

"Did you have sex with Benny on his honeymoon?"

Betsy was hurrying away, but she offered, "No! Yes! I said it's complicated! Leave me alone!"

"Benny was in his early twenties. How old were you?"

"Well life begins at forty and I was only forty three!"

"Would you say you were robbing the cradle? Why did you dress so 'young' today? How do you feel about Benny's comment that no sane person would touch you? Explain what you meant by 'baby I'm still a virgin'."

At that point, Sobers appeared to break up the interview, "Alright! That's enough! My client's had a tough day!"

Someone knocked on her door. Cathie rose lazily and went to pull it open. Benny came for comfort! She stepped back so he could enter inside her space.

"*Benny*!" She reached forth to give him a warm hug.

"Hi Cathie!" He walked into her reassuring arms.

"How are you holding up?"

"You're holding me up! I didn't want to go home and deal with Rochelle. I'm thinking of moving to another house that I bought years ago."

"See what she's up to first," she suggested. Then she added coyly and giggled "I have a large room upstairs!"

He laughed at her joke but he held on and squeezed her for consolation.

He warmed to her. She spoke in his ears "As I hold you now, it is impossible for someone somewhere else to have you. Rochelle held you on your honey moon. Nothing Betsy says adds up. Did you donate to a sperm bank Benny?"

"*No*!" he yelped like a man in pain.

"I will call your lawyer and you will tell him you need another DNA test. That one was compromised."

"I don't know! I'm losing the strength to fight!"

"I will fight when you are weak! Let's go! Let Mr. Barnaby attack this now!"

....

Rochelle cussed under her breath when the wiry woman claimed she met her. Then she recalled it! They were going for lunch on the second day. Betsy was in the hallway. She came to clean the room. She did remember greeting the woman.

Something was wrong with her story! If Rochelle could not remember anything else, she remembered Benny being with her all the time! How did he slip away to get with the Olive Oil woman?

If not for the DNA test she would disbelieve Betsy's story. Sneaky men would find ways to cheat! Maybe he did it as she slept! Jezebels like Betsy's were even sneakier! She was a virgin whore for crying out loud!

She would do what she would do when he was wide awake! She knew she could not take *everything*! She would take Benny Jnr. and his tattooed *essentials*! Even at that point, she would give him time to apologize. After the divorce, she would still wait for him to man up! Then anything that happened would be on him!

She loved him. That was a problem! She needed no one to tell her what to do. He hired a hot-looking bitch as an advisor! Rochelle did not trust that she-devil! She saw how Cathie looked at him! Jealousy to overcome was her biggest challenge now!

With what he did with Betsy, she did not trust him with Cathie! Why did it matter if she was leaving him?

Meanwhile, her parents were on their way home. All they wanted to do then was get drunk. Soon there would be no Benny to buy the liquor! Rochelle and her stupid pride would rob them of him. She was witchy when she spoke to them the last time! She planned to leave him but not to take her fair share and go! If she divorced him it would divorce them too!

Eric knew she was wrong about most of her claims. She coined a reality out of rage, spite and Holly Wood. She knew better than what she said. It was to punish Benny. She would punish herself! They, the parents, would be utterly punished! Rochelle was stiff-necked!

The Bensons were not perturbed! If Rochelle went through with her threat life would be hard for her family. Benny, being the great celebrity, would take it better than she would. West Keyes would not hate him! The nine-day wonder would pass. It would not be easy for Rochelle and her tattoo! It would torment her like Chucky up her ass!

The Bensons did not dwell on it. It would work out fine one way or the other. They would dwell on the good news that they had Bentley again. He was their grandson! They were hooked on him!

Milton Sobers sat in his make-shift home office doing paperwork and feeling important. Betsy came through after all! He had several live interviews on radio and television coming up. He would use these breaks to sell himself as a champion for women's causes against dead beat baby fathers. He would become an elite lawyer in West Keyes. He was doing fine so far.

He planned his final attack on Benny. He was a top fan of the celebrity but not a fan of the dead beat. He would get Betsy her retroactive payments. He would make Benny do well by her! By doing all that good, Milton would hit the mother lode - Cash! Everyone knew him as the hero! He was a celebrity now!

....

Fay Ambrose, Jennifer and Cassandra watched Betsy's interview. Fay saw disbelief on their faces. Did Betsy sleep with him? The evidence was clear!

"If that test didn't prove it, nothing could convince me that she slept with Benny Benson!" Cassandra stated matter-of-factly, unable to conceal her jealousy.

"It's unbelievable!" Jennifer agreed, "At her age her damned womb should have dried up! Imagine he was on his honeymoon with Rochelle. How did she do that?"

A thought struck Fay! She seemed baffled. Involuntarily, she exclaimed "*Bombo-claat*!"

When she realized her outburst the girls were already in her face. Reluctantly, she offered "The day when I left to check on her *something* happened!"

"You caught her with Benny?" Cassandra asked with fearful intense curiosity.

"Oh *please*! He never plugged his dick into Olive Oil!"

"What happened then?" Jennifer interjected, "Immaculate conception?"

Cassandra giggled at Jennifer's sarcasm. They eyed each other and broke out laughing. Fay did not join the ridiculous fit. They would soon laugh at her absurdity! Betsy did perform the scientifically impossible! That crazy joke came close to describing it. If the truth was the incredible anomaly how would you tell it? Instead of making them ridicule she made them laugh!

Fay giggled, "*Yes. Immaculate Conception.* You heard what she said – *'Baby I'm still a virgin!'*"

"Move your *bombo-claat* Flago!" Cassandra rebuked, imitating Fay.

"Did angels message Olive Oil?" Jennifer asked sarcastically. Fay was oblivious to her. She was back in that awful moment. They saw the horror on her face! She spoke! "Be real girls! What would it take for Benny Benson's dick to stand up when that slimy bitch is giving the goose pimples?"

"A miracle!" they said.

"I have *bad* memories on my mind right now!"

That day Fay walked inside the bathroom. Betsy was in the tub. She used the handle of a teaspoon to turn out a used condom. Then with the long stick handle on a West Keyes' flag, she inserted it, with the semen, well up inside her! It was revolting! That stick had to be too long! The beautiful flag was blowing by the strong wind coming from the fan.

Fay cussed and slapped her in the back of her neck. She never thought that Betsy's 'strategy' made any sense. She expected it to end where and when it started. It was an impossible thing that a dumb ass would do! Nine years later, the dumb ass act proved so effective, it fooled everyone!

Fay pitied Benny. He was innocent. She could not help him! What if she told the impossible story? Benny was fucked although he fucked no one but Rochelle!

She walked away with the Keys to Betsy's Toyota Corolla that day. Betsy would do anything to save her image and her job. Fay took the bribe to feather her own nest. She never imagined that Betsy's doing would come to hurt anyone. Now it tore one family apart!

Cassandra snapped her fingers at Fay, "Wake up!"

Fay came back to the moment facing curious eyes poking questions at her. Jennifer said, "Immaculate Conception is a tall tale my friend! You must have something better. Tell us!"

"You don't want to hear!" Fay cautioned.

....

Her worthless brother Christopher visited that day! They hardly spoke since he shacked up with Marlene.

"Christopher! Is that *you*? Why are you talking in a girl's voice?"

"That's his real voice now!" Marlene explained. "He came from jail with it! Now everyone in Rochester is asking *'who tamed that nigger?'* *'Who tamed that nigger?'* My man's been wrongfully and maliciously effeminized! It's embarrassing!"

"He fucking deserved it!" Rochelle screamed.

Back in the days, Marlene was her best friend second to Benny. The last time she saw Christopher she was eighteen in college. That day Benny Benson applied the fisticuffs and fixed him good!

The gigolo came to her room for 'a favor'. He said an American guest at some ABNB wanted 'a product' for fifty American dollars. "The problem is," he explained, "I do not have the 'exact' product that he would like. If you would sell him the product for me we could split the fifty. I would give you half Sis!"

He was so excited about half of fifty bucks! She wondered if the US dollar had infinite spending power.

"I don't know what you're talking about 'a product'! What product, Christopher?"

He took a deep breath and explained, "I only have *'a bottom'* but he wants *'a front'* for fifty. Help me Sis!"

Rochelle tore her eyes wide and screamed "Get out of my room faggot brother! Sell your own product and stop fucking begrudging mine!"

Christopher lunged at her! She shifted to the side avoiding him. He crashed face down on the couch. Rochelle slipped by swiftly and charged out the door. As she dashed outside she saw his guest standing in the way waiting for the product. He had the audacity to bring his 'client' along! She would not take any more of his abuse. She went for her own *ammunition*!

Rochelle ran across the East-Side lawn and screamed at the top of her voice, "Benny!"

She looked back. Christopher was catching up! Then Benny came full speed, charging by her with his big body. He crashed into Christopher hoisting him in the air. Christopher fell on his back, saw Benny's big bone knuckles and screamed in advance. The tourist quietly subtracted himself from the equation.

Benny snapped, "I told you to stop hitting your sister! Stop hitting your sister!"

As he spoke, he punctuated with knuckle punches. That was the last time Christopher disrespected her. Now he and Marlene were literally on their knees in her living room begging her not to leave Benny.

"You have nothing to lose? We haven't even seen you two in years!"

"Not so!" Marlene informed her. "We see Benny often. He takes care of us. After Christopher went to jail, I called him to help with 'a little donation' and he came. Christopher apologized to him. He sends us a little help every now and again. How will we survive if you break our bond?"

"I have my own Problems Marlene! I warned you about this gigolo! I bet he beats crap out of you!"

"No Rochelle! He doesn't hit anymore. When he went to jail they owned him too much! Ninety percent of his ego got blown out!"

Rochelle looked at Christopher expecting outrage. Christopher just knelt dear listening without a word.

"Don't let one little tattoo make you go insane," Marlene pleaded, "I live with the same thing too!"

"What do you mean?"

Marlene turned to Christopher, "Stand up bitch!"

He rose timidly. She stood up, unbuckled and unzipped his pants. "Be a good boy and turn around!"

Christopher turned bashfully. Marlene drew down his trousers. There it was, on his butt cheeks, the tattoo of a male name *PABLO DON*.

"Oh *shit*!" Rochelle exclaimed bewildered.

"How did you know?" Marlene asked, surprised.

"How did I know what?"

"About *the shit*! He was dripping all day when he came! I had to cork him up with tampons!"

"Oh hell I'm sorry!" Rochelle replied with sympathy.

"Oh god it's so painful! He only spent five nights in jail but he came back so fucking owned! Please don't give up on Benny! We need help! Benny's going to buy me a hair dressing parlor!"

6

Nicky Tats looked at his handiwork with proud approval. "There you go Miss Frazier! It's big and bold for you!" He handed the mirror to her. "What do you think?"

Betsy stared down at her crotch, smiling. "I love big and bold!" she beamed, "I hope it's bigger than *hers*?"

"Bigger than *whose*?" he asked looking puzzled.

"Rochelle Benson's of course!"

He put up his hand, shook his head and cleared his throat to opt out of that drama! He did what she requested. He would not dabble in other people's affairs. Benny never owned up to the child much less the mother but she was wearing his tattoo! It was not in Betsy's place to match tattoos with the wife!

She grabbed the mirror and took a second look. Nicky studied her. He was happy she was satisfied. She could not compete with Rochelle Benson! Betsy was narrow on all sides. If he had to do Benny's entire passport front page on her he would have to shrink it much. It would still spread from a narrow puff to narrow thighs!

Rochelle was not big or fat. She had crazy curves and bulges to tattoo on. She was impossibly sexy! Benny Benson was drunk or insane to look at Betsy!

Betsy was excited! She claimed she did it for Benny! Benny desperately did not want it! Since she had no one else to tell, she dialed Sobers on her way home.

"Hello. Milton Sobers here."

"Hello, Mr. Sobers. It's me!"

"Great!" he said, masking irritation. Betsy called him for everything that did not concern attorney work! "I know it is you Miss Betsy. How must I help you today?"

"I called to tell you I got my tattoo and it's good!"

"You do not need a tattoo for the case Miss Frazier."

"I don't?"

"*No!* Tattoos have nothing to do with child support?"

She paused to think and then said, "How *nothing*? This tattoo is important! I must compete!"

"With whom and for what?"

"I'm competing with Rochelle, remember?"

"No Miss Frazier. I do not remember. I am not a lawyer to help women compete with other women. You got a tattoo and good for you!"

"Thanks Mr. Sobers! I think it's good for me too!"

She paused to let him speak. He said nothing!

"*Mr. Sobers*?"

"Yes, *Miss Frazier*?"

"You didn't ask me what's on it!"

"What's on what?"

"On my *'privates'*!"

"No, I wouldn't ask!"

"You wouldn't? Why not?"

Sobers did not answer her. She offered, "I tattooed 'Benjamin Bentley Benson' on it! Mine is big and bold. It's well done!"

"Good for you! Now you can compete while I get back to work!"

"Ok, and thanks for the compliment!"

"*'The compliment'*?"

"Yes! You said it's good for me!"

"OK! That *compliment*. Have a nice day Miss Frazier!"

Betsy drove and whistled her way home. She went inside and turned on the television as if afraid to miss *anything*. Rochelle was on an interview! "*News flash* bitch!" Betsy yelled at the screen, patting her groin. "You have nothing on me now!"

She grabbed a bag of chips and sat watching.

Reporter: "Mrs. Benson. How is your relationship with the big man now that the case against him is proven?"

Rochelle: "Nothing good to tell you! One apology could fix everything but it's not forthcoming!"

Reporter: "That's unfortunate."

Rochelle: "Very unfortunate!"

Betsy chipped in, "Fortunate for me though, *bitch*!"

Reporter: "But he is still in the grace period of two weeks that you gave him to make the apology."

Rochelle: "Yes, he is. But he told me not to wait! He said he will never apologize for what he did not do!"

Reporter: "Even though it's been proven?"

Rochelle: "Yes. He's stuck on a lie!"

Reporter (Whistling with incredulity): "I know how you feel. You said the tattoo makes it worse. How much of a tattoo is it – Is it just his name?"

Rochelle (Rolling her eyes skyward for emphasis): "It includes the front page of his passport. That alone is a lot! It covers every space! And I'm not thin down there. He said it needed an ID. Benny is a possessive creature! So there's my dilemma!"

"*EEEHH*!" Betsy screamed, jumping from her seat and spilling chips! "She has his entire passport! That bitch! It's not fair!"

Betsy turned off the television and paced up and down for solutions. She called sobers again.

"Hello."

"Hello Mr. Sobers. It's me!"

"Sure Miss Frazier! I know it's you - again," he said, not able to suppress his tone.

"Are you watching Channel 9 on TV?"

"Sure, I am."

"Did you hear that audacious bitch?"

"*What*?"

"Did you hear what she said about the tattoo?"

"Well, sure I did."

Betsy paused. He was ready to hang up. She asked, "Can we obtain a copy of the front page of Benny's passport?"

"Why?"

"Because I have a child for the gentle man and I am entitled to him! I need it!"

"So how am I going to get it?"

"You're the lawyer. You tell me!"

"Well, maybe go and ask Benny. Or try to get a photo of Rochelle's puff !" he offered sarcastically.

"Great idea! Do that by Monday!"

Mr. Sobers hung up the phone!

....

Milton Sobers dressed like a charmer for the April 3rd hearing. Betsy bought a dress that seemed identical to what Rochelle wore the last time, except that it was a knock off. She did not look 'exactly' like Rochelle in it!

Sobers went to pick her up. She came out! What he saw was befuddling but he made no mention of it. He composed himself and asked, "Are you ready to shake him down?"

"Yes! He's all mine! His tattoo makes me so confident!"

"Good! We should raise you a tidy sum off this one!" the stocky little man paused to reflect. Then he added with ridiculous sarcasm, "I hope he stays as rich as he is. Rochelle Benson threatens to magically take over half of his wealth after the divorce!"

Betsy's eyes lit up with desperate urgency. "*EEEEHH!* Well can I have the other half? Can we take all of it before she gets any?"

He was about to laugh before realizing that she was dead serious. He frowned and asked, "*What*?"

"You're not listening! I said I want all or half!"

"How could you expect half his estate? You're not even the man's wife! You were never his wife! Not even she can get that much! I was joking Miss Betsy."

"Never mind! When Benny marries me I'll have it all!"

At that point, he looked at her again and said, "I see you dressed to impress."

"Since *everyone* wants to show cleavages and curves! I'm here to show them that they're not good enough!"

"I surmise that *everyone* means Rochelle."

"Yes, it does!"

He scratched his head and offered, "For some folks, simplicity is wisdom. Wisdom is simplicity!"

"*I know*!" she chirped "The simpler the better!"

"Do you ever live by your belief?" he quizzed.

"What did you say?"

"Never mind! Just don't talk inside the courthouse!"

Betsy did not expect Rochelle to turn up! She wanted the opportunity to be the hottest thing in court. That *bitch* came looking hotter than before!

"Why is she always turning up?" Betsy agitated, "Is she tailing me?"

"This case is important to her," Sobers replied coolly.

"What happens between my baby father and me is none of her damned business!" Betsy agitated.

"Not when the baby father is her husband," Sobers advised.

"Who's her husband?" she questioned skeptically, "She doesn't even want him! I'm the only love he has!"

They were still outside. Rochelle heard what Betsy said and went to confront her! "Stop making mischief *Olive Oil*! Haven't you done enough home wrecking?"

Betsy backed off wary of the venom that an angry Rochelle packed. Mother Benson came to lead her daughter-in-law away. "Come with me sugar!"

They walked off and Betsy shouted "I have my Benny Benson tattoo too! His mother will be mine soon!"

Rochelle froze. Mother Benson pushed her behind her and went to Betsy. "Stop playing bigger than your size old woman! Look at my daughter-in-law and then look at you! Don't you see you're not cutting it?"

"I'm cutting it too!" Betsy retorted. She turned to Sobers, "Tell her Milton! Tell her that I'm cutting it!"

Suspicious eyes circled to the attorney. An attorney client relationship would seem in bad taste. "I know *nothing!*" he asserted for all to know. The people surmised that Betsy was insane and slutty and Sobers was pushing his own agenda to milk Benny!

7

When the court was called to order Judge Maria Mason was smiling. Betsy Frazier's case against Benny Benson felt personal to her! It was not that he was a dead beat dad – although that contributed to the disgust! It was the *peripheral* matter! He gave Rochelle that tattoo and then cheated on her! She wanted revenge against him! Some other chap did a tattoo thing to another woman! It would be easy as A-B-C!

Milton Sobers approached the judge with Betsy. "Hello Your Honor!" the wiry woman called. "It's me!"

"I see that it's you Miss Frazier," Maria said soberly.

Benny insisted that he was not the father after the test proved otherwise. His attorney alluded to having concerns about the paternity test being compromised! Everybody knew who Bentley Benson's father was by mere visual alone! Everyone except the papa and his lawyer! It irritated Maria immensely!

She saw how ridiculous it was but allowed his lawyer to have his say. She listened refusing to reprimand those who laughed at intervals. Be it inside the courthouse or not, it was understandable! Maria smiled pitifully at the lawyer. "Life as an attorney can be *that* hard, Mr. Barnaby! You must find it impossible to believe what you are saying but...you took the case, didn't you?"

"I have no doubt that my client is telling the truth Your Honor," Barnaby croaked unconvincingly and then cleared his throat.

Judge Maria watched Benny who was decked in his expensive attire. He looked like he thought he owned the world and all the tattooed women! She saw his wife watching him and shared her disgust! Maria translated her solidarity with a sisterly nod.

She turned to the victim. Poor lanky little woman! How much Betsy had to bear for Benny Benson's amusement. Awful men! He made her rob his cradle! He should be ashamed of himself! Thank goodness she was strong enough to survive. Maria felt pity for her. She could harm no one! She was not nicely dressed. That was impossible for her but she wore appropriate attire. Benny Benson used her and dropped her inside the bowl like toilet paper! He flushed her off! Now he wanted to flush away the child too! Maria Mason would make things right!

Benny Benson monster could not say that Maria did not give him justice. She gave him the benefit of an impossible doubt! She allowed him another DNA test to prove a lame case. She knew it would prove the opposite! She would read the result last!

Attorney Barnaby said "Your Honor, I tell you with no doubt in my mind that my client does not know this woman who claims to have his child. She is an impostor! Mr. Benson never had sex with her and *cannot* be her child's father."

Judge Maria Mason cackled raucously. A chorus of laughter followed from the packed audience. She tolerated it, smiling and waiting for it to seize.

"Is Mr. Benson lying to this court?" she asked with raw rhetoric.

"Surely not, Your Honor," Barnaby asserted for the umpteenth time, sounding exhausted.

"Should the result of the second paternity test prove otherwise, will he admit to being the father?"

"He will not lie to you Your Honor!"

"I will not take an impossible denial lightly! Miss Frazier claims she got pregnant by your client at the time of his honey moon, when he took his wife to the hotel where she worked. Does your client remember honey-mooning at the West Keyes Hotel?"

"Sure Your Honor."

"And does he remember her coming to his room?"

"No Your Honor! It was nine years ago. They had no contact to give him cause to remember her by."

She turned to Rochelle and asked her to approach the bench. Rochelle came and stood beside Benny.

"Mrs. Benson, do you remember seeing this woman at the time of your honey moon nine years ago?"

"Vaguely, Your Honor. We were going out. She was coming to tidy our room. That was the only time I saw her. It was on our last day at the hotel."

"Your husband says he does not remember her at all! She and an unquestionable paternity test claim him to be her child's father!"

"I know, Your Honor. That's a *strange* denial!"

Judge Mason guffawed. "It is *strange* Mrs. Benson!"

Rochelle muttered beneath her breath, "Men who make impossible denials should be castrated!"

Benny looked at her in shock. Rochelle locked eyes with him and smiled spitefully. Maria gave the woman a cheeky look, "What did you say dear? Oh – don't bother to answer that! Whatever you said you said!"

She made a telepathic connection with Rochelle and continued, "Did you suspect that your husband was having contact with Miss Frazier?"

"Not at all, Your Honor. She's old for him too...like a cradle robber! She has that Olive Oil thing going on! I would not believe she was his type!"

Betsy did a three sixty degree spin for all to see how ridiculous Rochelle's insult was. Everyone laughed! Maria took of her glasses, eyed Betsy and then ignored.

Maria cleaned her glasses and put them back on. "How old are you Miss Frazier?"

"She is fifty one Your Honor."

"Fifty one," Maria pondered. "She was definitely old for him then! Mr. Benson would be twenty-three at the time. She's over fifty today and he is just thirty-two. *Wow!*" She added sarcastically, "You go *old girl*! Cradle robber or not, she broke no law!"

"She was no cradle robber," Sobers interjected, "They were both adults, Your Honor."

"Yap-yap-yap Mr. Sobers!" Maria snapped "No one said he was a minor!"

She turned to Barnaby. "Is your client ready for the result of the test he did at a lab of his choice?"

"Yesterday Your Honor!" Barnaby asserted to a round of mocking laughter.

She took off her glasses and caught Benny's eyes with disbelief, "You are a bold man, Mr. Benson. I give you that! I am anxious to read it too, but first, let us listen to what Miss Frazier is demanding from you…I mean, based on the claim that you are a delinquent parent! You will listen to these demands, Mr. Benson, and if this test absolves you – which it won't – you will behave yourself and be a man. You will make the necessary redress. I will teach you what being a man means…and you will pay dearly! I hope that when your wife is ready for you, I will be at this bench to assist her to enlighten you as well! You were a twenty-three year old spoiled brat and at thirty-two, you still are!"

She gestured to Milton Sobers, "Take us back through the whole thing, starting from the beginning at West Keyes Resort. Then state what your client is rightfully demanding. Let us see if it will jog Mr. Benson's memory!"

The stocky attorney cleared his throat to begin. "Thank you, Your Honor! As you said, my client met Mr. Benson at the West Keyes Hotel, where she had sexual contact with him. It turned out that she got pregnant, which she discovered weeks later…"

"And did she contact Mr. Benson about her pregnancy?" the judge asked with a frown.

"My client tried your honor. She used a phone number that she obtained from him at the hotel. When she tried to tell him he hung up the phone."

"He hung up the phone and then what?"

"She tried a number of times, Your Honor. She could not get through to him. At one point she decided to try raising the child by herself. Fortunately, the law in our country still allows the mother to state the father's name for the birth certificate. She registered him with his right name – Benson I mean."

"OK…So she decided to raise the child on her own! Why is she here now?"

"It was not really a choice Your Honor. She had to! When Bentley became eight a few months ago, he kept crying and asking for his dad. She told him all the great stories about Mr. Benson. He in turn would go to school and tell his friends. They would mock him, saying that he was a Benny Benson bastard. In addition to that, it became too expensive to continue raising a child by herself. Several months ago she discovered where his mansion was. She made a visit. His wife, Mrs. Rochelle Benson intimidated and scared her away!"

At his last sentence, Rochelle screamed from her corner, "*Oh God*! She never came to the hou…!"

"Mrs. Benson!" Judge Mason cautioned, "Don't let me have to throw you out!"

She turned back to the attorney, "Now please continue, Mr. Sobers. Tell us what she is asking for."

"Miss Frazier is simply demanding what is rightfully due to her. Nine years of neglect by Benny Benson should amount to nine years of child support and other expenses, which my client had to stick out on her own. In addition to that, she will require child support going forward. We would calculate her retroactive nine years of support at the rate of what the court decides is the reasonable weekly rate of support for Bentley."

"OK – I understand!" the Judge replied, "We will calculate what he owes when we figure out how much he should be paying from day one. Then there is the matter of her nine months pregnancy – which you are also claiming for at the value of one year. That I don't follow, Mr. Sobers! Well, since she had lost much time, effort and some cash in the period when he was avoiding her, we could consider compensation – and that includes the period when he failed to support her before Bentley was born. I do not know about one year retroactive payment for that though!"

She paused and took up the envelope in front of her, "Benny Benson has some money! Everyone is going to want lots of it now – Right? I have to consider what is reasonable for child support...and I have to consider the fact that this child deserves the full right as does his sibling. I hold a strong view that Benny Benson's hard earned money is Benny Benson's hard earned money! Take that however you all like! I have been in this bench for quite some time and seen it all! I am for justice, but I will give the devil his due too!"

Mario rifled through the envelope. "None of the above will be relevant until we prove that Bentley Benson is Benny Benson's son!" She eyed Mr. Sobers teasingly, "Right, Mr. Sobers?"

"That's right Your Honor," Sobers agreed nervously.

"Stop jittering Mr. Barnaby! You're just the attorney! Here is unquestionable proof either way. Bentley Benjamin Benson *is certainly* the son of Benjamin Bentley Benson! Now we have put this thing to rest!"

Benny seemed to lose his balance. Attorney Barnaby reached out to hold him up. Rochelle screamed something that sounded like *'fucking pig'*, but Judge

Mason did not notice. She was confused, trying to figure out their names. Maybe it was a typing error. "Mr. Sobers," she asked with a frown, "What is Bentley's full name…because I think that there is an error here."

"His name is Bentley Benjamin Benson, Your Honor."

"No way! That's his father's name!"

"No Your Honor! His Father is Benjamin Bentley Benson."

"So…It is the same names turned differently. Like…he's Benjamin Jnr. – or *'sort of'*!"

"*No* Your Honor!" Rochelle yelled, "*My* son is Benjamin Jnr!"

"Oh, calm down please! I am too confused to be yelled at, Mrs. Benson!"

Betsy Frazier chipped in, "The names are correct, Your Honor. I did not want any conflict. The boys were born the same day. I heard the news that Rochelle would name her son by *my* Benny's name! I turned them around to prevent problems in the future!"

"I see," the judge replied scratching her head, "'*Your Benny's name*' was actually *her husband's name*, to which his legitimate child *was entitled*. So now we have three people with the same names! You created the problem by avoiding it Miss Betsy! It is confusing!"

"My Bentley was entitled to his father's name too, Your Honor!"

"I did not say he was not entitled to his father's name! His father was supposed to decide! You should not have! It is audacious!" She turned to Rochelle, "I understand the boy spends much time with Mr. Benson's parents, which Mr. Benson does not approve of. Am I right?"

"Yes, Your Honor! They try to correct his crooked ways but the devil is the devil!"

"I see. Did Mr. Benson's mother know that the child – just like his brother, had all Mr. Benson's names?"

"I'm sure not, Your Honor. We knew he was Bentley. We assumed that his middle name was different."

"Well you all assumed wrongly! Mr. Benson is the proud and not so proud father of 'Junior' and 'Junior'!"

Benny fainted. No one noticed, except Attorney Barnaby…and Betsy Frazier who lamented, "My poor Benny just fainted! Let me help you darling!"

"Shut up Olive Oil!" Rochelle screamed, "You need to change those names!"

Judge Maria eyed both women curiously, allowing them to argue the point and bring more disorder to the court. More drama could only help her equilibrium!

"*My* son is more important than *yours*!" Betsy told Rochelle, "He's just like Benny! You can't deny him Benny's name! The other boy can't even run! Name him after you! My boy will make me rich – *BOOM*!"

As Betsy spoke she hustled to check on Benny. Maria pointed her back to her place. Rochelle was going to Betsy but mother Benson pulled her back.

"Behave yourselves, Mrs. Benson and you Miss Frazier!" Maria ordered in a devilish tone. She added "I see your pain Mrs. Benson but *hold* it! Let me finish this case, forget the craziness and go home!"

She turned to Attorney Barnaby, "Will your client rise to hear the rest and put off fainting until later? It gets worse, as you both should know!"

"He will rise, Your Honor."

"Good! I will not speak until he stands up! If he does not, it will be for contempt of court in my book!"

Attorney Barnaby nudged the athlete and helped him up. Benny stood in a daze but he was hearing well enough! He shook his head defiantly! "Lie, lie, lie!"

"That's what we feared!" Judge Mason affirmed disgustedly, "The impossible denial!"

"And the wicked oaths too!" Rochelle chipped in, "Like swearing that God's thunder should break his neck if he was lying!"

Maria Mason took off her glasses, wiped it and put it back on. "Mr. Benson, we will finish this matter in three week's time, on the twenty-ninth of this month! Mean time, you *will* pay child support at a value of eight hundred dollars weekly! You were delinquent for four hundred and sixteen weeks. You must pay Miss Frazier three hundred and thirty two thousand dollars plus legal expenses for this case! I will decide on her additional claims and tell you on our next date! You say the boy is not yours. I say that if you do not pay you will be locked in jail for a long time! Be good Mr. Benson. Remember the women you impregnate! Make sure no other child is out there with all your names! Please do not challenge God to break your neck! He might oblige!"

Judge Mason paused. Betsy Frazier stood with her hand raised like a kindergarten kid.

"What is it, Miss Frazier?" Maria asked annoyed.

"Your Honor, I hear that Rochelle will take My Benny to court for half of his property."

"What business is that of ours, presumptuous woman?" Maria agitated amidst all the chuckling.

"It's my business too! I deserve the other half!"

"*What woman?*"

"I'll have to take care of him when she leaves him...and I have Bentley to..."

"Betsy Frazier! You're *stressing* me out!" She brought down the hammer and said, "No more dumb questions! The court is dismissed! Get out of my sight!"

Betsy left reluctantly. She looked over her shoulder. Rochelle was coming, shoes in hand! Mother Benson pulled Rochelle back. Betsy took off! Maria Mason sat watching intensely, hoping that Rochelle would catch up to Betsy! It was wrong for a judge, but..!

Benny still stood at the bench waiting for the dream to end. Barnaby grabbed his elbow pulling him backward. Benny came to his senses and saw that it was no dream! He fainted again...

The bailiff stepped over him and addressed Maria, "*What a day!*" he mused, glancing over his shoulder to the judge, before telling all to rise. Maria smiled guiltily, "These days make me more human!"

He chuckled, "I noticed it triggered your emotions, Your Honor!"

"And those include the bad ones!"

....

Rochelle drove Mother Benson to her house, picked up Benny Jnr. from his grandfather and sped home with fixity of purpose. There was one thing to do at that time! She wished he made it harder for her!

He was not just a liar. He was a dirty scumbag of a liar! The only liar next to him would be his mistress Betsy! She had the audacity to lie that Rochelle threatened her at the house! She never saw that fiddle-foot devil since they 'half met' at the Clair-Castle! Had it not been for the paternity test, her astonishing lie would make Rochelle disbelieve everything she said! Although that would still be hard! You only had to look at Bentley to know who his father was!

She drove into the yard. He was waiting. He parked on the lawn and stood beside his expensive AMG. She parked inside the garage. He came behind her BMW! She was about to reverse on him but she remembered Benny Jnr. in the back. He did not wait until she came out. He pulled the door open for her, unaware that his son was in the back. She hissed! He could easily forget his own flesh and blood! Rochelle slammed the door back shut and reopened it for herself. "Get your son! Dead beat son-of-a-bitch!" she screamed at him. She realized what she said and retracted, "My apologies to Mother Benson! How you are her son I don't know!"

He pulled the door open for the boy, "Here Benny. Let's go, son!"

Benny Jnr. jumped from the car gleefully. Then worry appeared on his face. "What is it?" Benny asked.

"Are you a dead beat son-of-a-bitch Dad?"

He wanted to say 'no' but he did not know what Rochelle would do. He walked away. Rochelle grabbed Benny Jnr's shoulder. "No son! He's your father! I'm stressed out, so I said a bad thing!"

"I understand Mom! If I get stressed out and say something…you won't punish me?"

She seemed confused. Did he ask a question or make a statement? Finally, she offered, "I'm sorry Benny Jnr. I won't say that again! No one should say it when they're stressed out – OK?"

"If I call someone a dead beat son-of-a-bitch, I will say sorry and then I will not say it again – OK Mom?"

She did not answer him and he repeated "OK Mom?"

"*No*! It's not *OK*! Just don't say it in the first place!"

"Right! I will say it after he pisses me off!"

She left the argument alone! He was a little Benny coming up! He was hard to out talk but he did not show the lying symptoms. To be fair, Benny never showed anything remotely dishonest until Betsy Frazier popped up from hell or somewhere like it!

Benny waited at the front door. Benny Jnr. pushed past him and Rochelle allowed him to go inside. Benny opened his mouth to speak. She wagged a finger at his lips, "Wait! Are you about to apologize?"

"No Rochelle, but listen, I..."

"Give it up scumbag! I don't want to hear it then!"

He stopped talking and turned to go in.

"I will allow you inside. Stay no longer than it will take to pack your belongings! You must go! Now!"

"This is *my* house! I wasn't even married to you when I built it!"

"So are you throwing out Benny Jnr. and me?"

"No Rochelle...I...I..."

"*Good*! Now one of us has to go!"

"All right Rochelle," he replied hoarsely, "I will go!" He added defiantly "I will be damned if I apologize!"

"*Fine*! Don't be damned for me and your son!"

"Woman you don't know that you're talking *shit*!"

"Me and the old world knows *you're* talking *shit*!"

8

He had a place to go but the emptiness made it seem cold. Since the day it began he was lonely. Great Benny was a solitary on a checkered chess board. He had to be far from people; just not too far from the one person who held him up. She jokingly offered an extra room to him. He had a second mansion but Cathie's place was far more welcoming…

Rochelle was his biggest pain which he was not aware of until that moment. The only people he had on his side were his son Benjamin and Cathie. He could tolerate his parents and hers but they turned him off too – always trying to convince him to apologize for nothing. It was better to avoid them! He wished he could take his son with him but that was another pain he would come to accept. Life as it used to be was over.

He would get over it and start again. He would take Benny! He would find a woman and move on. He felt like the woman of the future was already there waiting for him to be ready! There was everything about her!

At 10:49 PM she was in bed watching old Benny Benson races on YouTube. Once upon a time, her fantasy was to stand in his presence for once in her life and get to know him. That was before he married his best friend Rochelle. Now she had a new fantasy and she was not ashamed of it.

Cathie was a decent child who believed that people should get what they deserved! Rochelle did not deserve him anymore! It would be bad to see him with a broken family – especially since a child was involved. Still, it was what it was. It did not take much to see that as impossible as the entire affair sounded, Benny was not lying! He needed support. She was willing to give him that for everything in return. If it made her a bad person then so be it! Rochelle made her own decision!

When he approached her about being his advisor, she felt that it was unnecessary. When she realized the gravity of the situation, especially with Rochelle spitting venom, she felt he made a wise decision. She thanked god that she was his choice.

She remembered on the second day of meeting him, talking to her sister and explaining why she believed he was not lying about the Betsy Frazier incident. Her sister laughed so hard it was embarrassing. She knew what Benny was feeling. His truth seemed impossible to fathom much less prove. What was going on? How could this woman have a child that had his DNA without sleeping with him? She dozed off in her thoughts and dreamed about things concerning Benny Benson. She kissed him in her dreams...

He was parked in her yard at 10:49 PM, wondering if it was a good idea. He sought to embarrass himself for a room at this woman's house when he had a whole mansion in a nearby district...too far from his community, too far from Benny Jnr. and too far from the wonderfully loyal Cathie Crew!

He bit his lips and pressed down on his horn. He was already there. He would just make a fool of himself and get it over with. She said it as a joke but he played like he believed her. It was late. She was an early sleeper. He played like he did not know. He held the horn under sustained pressure, not caring about her neighbors!

It startled Cathie out of her sleep. She thought the burglar alarm went off. Then she remembered that she had none at home. That annoyance was at work! She jumped up in a hurry and went to the window that overlooked her front lawn. The beautiful AMG was there! The top was pulled off. She looked down at him in the middle of a bundle of belongings. A surge of joy swept through her entire body! "Oh my God!" she mused in disbelief, "He accepted my offer! Gee, I must be somebody to him!"

Benny was still making noise, oblivious to her looking down at him.

She drew the window and put her hand out to wave. He let go off the horn and waved back.

Cathie drew away from the window and flew out the room door and down the stairs, fearing she would fall…

He saw her hand move away and hopped out of the car. Benny began to take his belongings out. He placed them onto her front porch. She had to be saying yes, because he was not going to be turned away for a second time that night!

....

She did not want to lose him but she had to know he cared. That was why she needed the apology. They were best friends since high school and the bond that held them together was stronger than that of the ordinary couple. At some point she would have to give in. She did not want to seem so desperate that he could walk all over her pride.

She was hard but it was justifiable. He got a strange woman pregnant! That was worse! She was not even treating him as his sins deserved! Well, she kicked him out, so maybe she was! She was now in pain wanting him to come back home! She felt too damned weak! Rochelle Georgia Benson was a punk out pussy! She threw him out last night and she was going there this morning to see that he was there! Was she still playing the wife's roll? Why should she be doing that?

She took a glance at her alibi Benny Jnr. She was bringing him to see his father as he was sleeping when he left. Rochelle placed her knuckles to her lips and yawned. She never knew that Beardsley Manor was so far from their village! After forty five minutes driving she was bored.

The house came to view and a strange nervousness came over her. "That's my house Mom!" Benny Jnr. yelled excitedly.

"*Your* house?"

"Yes Mom! Dad told me so! It's beautiful like yours and I love it – I love it!"

"*Nice,*" she replied choked up. Benny was a bastard but sometimes that bastard was so sweet! It was why she could not leave him the heck alone! Who on earth made everyone feel good? When he bought that house she never knew it was for little Benny! He bought it the day the boy was born! How could someone so perfect do so badly? Betsy Frazier could not seduce herself! What a crazy phenomenon!

They drove to the front gate and her heart leaped to her chest. He was not there! There was no sign of the AMG! It was just 6:51 in the morning. She did not sleep all night and her son was up from sometime after 5:00 AM. He came knocking at her room door to ask if he had returned.

Wherever Benny was, he would be wrapped in his sheet until 8:30 AM or so. Rich people that made their money on auto-pilot tended to enjoy more luxuries than others. Although she bossed him around, she had work to get to by 9:00 AM. He was still her boss! It was another proof of how nice he was. *'Nice'* was losing some flavor now! Where the fuck was he all night!

Screaming dirty images rushed to her cranium. She had no sex since the whole thing began! Now she saw him in her mind, naked as the day he was born, entangled between the wiry limbs of Betsy Frazier! No way! Scrap that! He could not have been with her!

She remembered Cathie, 'the *advisor*'! That was the most beautiful *bitch* she saw for a while! *"Jesus!"* she muttered, cussing beneath her breath.

"Yes Mom?" Benny Jnr. replied, thinking she was speaking to him.

"Not you there!" Rochelle backed up into the gateway in order to make a u-turn. Then she charged off down the road, blasting all cylinders with full capacity. The speed of acceleration pulled them back onto their seats like magnets. She was too intent on what she was doing to realize what she was doing. Benny Jnr. was in a horrific thrill, screaming "Ooohhhh!" going down the road...

Rochelle glanced at him through the rearview and said *"Ouch!"* Then she forgot what that was for and floored the accelerator again. If Benny did not resist Olive Oil, how on earth could he resist that smooth skinned beauty? She was driving but anxiety was killing her. She wanted to get there faster than fast! It could not be her business but she wanted to see!

As she drove by Cathie's house the AMG came to view! Benny was inside there! "Holy *fuck*!" she muttered, "What did I do? What did I fucking do?"

She remembered Benny Jnr. and looked to make sure he did not hear her. He was not listening but she watched him, thinking she betrayed him. Benny Benson was his life – and hers! She never had to work hard for anything! He made all possible! She only had to take care of his 'accumulations', which he did for them. Jealousy was making her more jealous and taking the love she had!

She said things to scare him as he did not know much about business. Now he had Cathie! He could take Benny Jnr from her and give her a little house and a token! She could not take him for what he was worth! That was bull shit! As his advisor she introduced him to prenuptials herself! She never envied his success. She wanted to give him something to worry about as punishment for his infidelity! Now she was worried!

Cathie woke up in the morning remembering *him*. She called downstairs to tell Simone, her maid, to get breakfast ready a little 'latish'. She was not going to the office that day. She smiled and turned onto her side to go back to sleep. Benny was not an early riser. She was more impressed with the man after last night! There was everything about him!

....

She was downhearted and pissed off that morning. When she pulled up at her gate there was a strange woman waiting. That alone was annoyance!

Rochelle eyed her. She was about five feet six inches and a hundred and forty pounds. She was a nicely curved young lady who knew how to wear her clothes. Rochelle wondered if she was another one from out of the wood-work!

The gate pulled open and she hesitated and wound down the window. As the woman approached her she said, "Yes ma'am?"

"Mrs. Rochelle Benson?"

"Yes," she replied ironically, "I'm still that for now!"

"*No!*" the woman retorted, "For the rest of your life you will be! You're not going to leave your husband!"

"What do you mean?"

"I know you don't remember me but you need to talk to me more than I need to talk to you, Mrs. Benson!"

"Why do you say that?"

She giggled, "Because I'm giving you the impossible truth to make you sure that Mr. Benson is innocent!"

"He cannot be innocent! That's his son!"

"You have tunnel vision! I didn't say it's not his son. Bentley is his son but he's one hundred percent innocent too! Freaky science! I'm here to *marvel* you!"

Rochelle thought and said "My mind tells me to send you away in anger but my gut says to indulge you. The gate is open! Please go on inside!"

The woman went and stood on her front porch. Rochelle came out of the car with the Keys and headed to the door. Benny took them from her and did the honors. She turned to the woman who reached out her hand and declared, "I'm Fay Ambrose! I've been working at Clair-Castle for ten years now. I know what happened to you and Mr. Benson."

"I'm confused right now…"

"I saw what happened and I'm still confused!"

"*Seriously*? Come inside Fay! You have an accent. Is it Jamaican?"

"Yes I am!"

"*Yah man*! I could tell! I love a Jamaican accent!"

"People say that a lot."

"If what you're saying is true, why would you want to help me? If it's money, Benny is the loaded one. I only work for him."

Fay ignored her words. "I had a ten minutes conversation with you on your honeymoon. I thought you were nice but I did not come to help you. I'm a Benny Benson fan like everyone else. Most of all, I don't like Betsy Frazier. I feel sorry for her still. She's a very foxy and mentally deranged individual."

"She's so evil that she seems crazy Fay!"

"I live with it every day!"

Rochelle laughed. Fay was a happy-go-lucky! She could help you to keep a light heart.

"Speaking of why I would help," Fay added, giggling "I got my first car because of Betsy and Benny Benson, which Benny Benson does not even know?"

"OK…So I'm assuming that's a riddle of sorts."

"It's no riddle. It's the confusing shit to explain! If it was normal you would not be in this mess. The truth is more unbelievable than a lie. Benny's problem is that he's the one telling it!"

"You're playing with my head! Tell me more!"

"I will!" she paused and questioned Rochelle. "Do you remember me yet? We spoke in the park on the last day of the honey moon."

Rochelle smiled, "The minute you said you worked at West Keyes I remembered you. Benny admired that you were always laughing and having fun with guests."

"I admired *you* on that day and now you're even more beautiful! Your husband is the last of his kind! Don't lose him!"

Rochelle laughed nervously. "Thanks for the kind words. I'm thinking you're hot and you're thinking the same about me! You saw me being jealous that day when Benny spoke about you. The thing with beauty is that no one has a monopoly on it. Right as we speak, my husband is finding shelter at a place where an even more beautiful gem resides!"

"That's a natural cause for panic but not a sensible one! Jealousy is natural but not sensible! Look on the bright side."

"I don't see that side! Where is it?" Rochelle quizzed.

"*Here*! If he does not do her, you know you have a better Benny than you thought! I already know!"

"That's how I felt months ago! Now he has no reason to restrain himself. He's sep..."

"I don't believe he's separated in his mind yet. He'll wait for a resolution first." Fay asserted confidently.

Fay giggled. Rochelle frowned. *"What?"*

"It's time to show you a video on my new Galaxy girl! I only use Galaxy so the picture is nice and clean!"

When Fay left that morning Rochelle pondered over the story. It seemed ridiculous from all angles. It was impossible every way she looked at it. It also seemed impossible that Benny found time to go anywhere at any time without her noticing! He was locked between her legs day and night! There was not a second when she was not with him! Did Betsy give Benny a hard on? How could she explain that? Only by accepting Fay's story. If she did she would be as laughable as Benny! She imagined telling it to the court. The judge would laugh to death! The laughter would stop when she showed the video!

Not everything that was true was admissible. Most people chose the lie and suffered the consequences of betraying the truth. When truth did not fall within the prescribed and preconceived notion of what was normal, the liar got the credibility. The truth only attracted ridicule! She ridiculed Benny!

Benny had no chance to physically go out to whore during that period. How did Bentley really happen?

....

She drove into the school yard. The AMG was parked to her left. Benny was dressed in full white and sunglasses. He did not see the BMW pull up a hundred feet from him. She could go straight inside with Benny Jnr., but she knew what he came for. She pulled Benny left of his track to the vehicle. The boy seemed puzzled until he saw it. "It's Daddy!" he yelled excitedly.

The roof was up and the windows closed. He did not hear the boy shout for him. He waited in confidence that he would catch them going inside!

She knocked on the window startling him. Benny saw them and wound it down. "Thanks Rochelle," he said bashfully.

"He has a home. You could see him there."

"I know. I don't want to come and argue."

"But you want to go to some bitch's place and do what...*fuck*?"

He looked at the boy indicatively and she covered her mouth with apology.

"There we go Rochelle! I won't respond to that!"

"I'm sorry Benny. It's frustrating!"

"I know. You're always jealous, but I'm not blaming you. It's that devil woman! I'm not blaming me either!"

She shook her head in agreement and walked off so he could talk to Benny Jnr. She stood at a distant watching them.

They said sons loved their mothers more. Benny Jnr. seemed the opposite. Her own parents showed more love to Benny than they showed her! He was just contagious! She was practical and grounded. People misunderstood her easily. The only time they misunderstood Benny was with this Betsy affair. If people loved her the way they loved him she would be thankful!

She looked at her watch and went back to the car. He told the boy to go off to school. Benny Jnr. went to the building. She paused at the side of his car. "Benny, you should consider coming to see him whenever you like."

"I never doubted that. I'm just avoiding…"

"*Me*?" she challenged, "Are you tired of me?"

"Rochelle, please don't!"

"*Oops*! Sorry again!" She paused and made sure to get it right this time. "Look, I met someone yesterday and I need to talk to you ab…"

"No, I can't talk about it! I'm tired o…"

"It's not about tha…"

"I can't talk about *anything* now! I'm sorry Rochelle."

"I see," she conceded with conspicuous reluctance. She fought to contain her tears and he waited for her to finish so he could go. He did not feel like being in that space with her. He loved Rochelle but he hated her energy these days. She was one of a nation of people trying to force him to sin against himself.

"Your house is yours and mine." She offered speculatively. "Benny Jnr's house does not belong to either of us. Come back to your home."

"It's only been two days since you threw me out!"

"I know and I was wrong. Come back! You don't have to apologize."

"But you have to believe me!" he emphasized. "That's the problem!"

He started the engine indicatively. Rochelle watched nervously, a confused disbelieving look on her face. "And does *she* believe you?"

He thought about her question. At first he did not know who she was talking about. When he realized that she was referring to Cathie, he said "Yes. She's the only one who believes me!"

He drove off. She was glued to the spot as if waiting for him to come back and explain. Then she realized her mistake. Jealousy got her again! She was concentrating on Cathie instead of the fact that she believed him now! That was all she had to say!

"This is how he felt when I was the hard case!" she mused bitterly, shaking her head. "*Fuck* karma!"

She remembered Benny Jnr. and looked to the gate. He went inside by himself.

Rochelle left the school yard peeling tires. She hit the high way, heading for Cathie Crews office! She parked outside in less than fifteen minutes. She did not stop to catch her breath. She barged in and stormed by the receptionist who hurried from her desk to stop her.

"Go sit down!" Rochelle ordered, pointing a warning finger at the confused girl.

"Please ma'am," the youngster protested. "I have to do my job!"

"I said sit down! I'm not here to rob or shoot anyone! Your job will be fine!"

She knew Rochelle Benson too well – Not personally but through the media. Rochelle was known to put women that came on to Benny through the shredder! He was the most stalked man on West Keyes Island and she was the most effective security system. Now the news going around said that Benny Benson was shacking up with Cathie Crew…her boss!

What would she do? Should she call the cops? Should she throw herself in the ring and get pulverized to keep a job? That would not be worth it. Rochelle had her between a rock and a hard place!

"A-Are you going to b-beat her up, Mrs. Benson?"

"Do I look like a barbarian to you? I don't fight!"

"Y-You d-d-don't f-fight?"

"I mean, on Mondays! What day is today?"

"I-It's Tuesday m-ma'am."

"Oh shit! The week goes fast! Fortunately I don't fight on Tuesdays either! There you have it! Now go sit down and behave yourself! Unless you're trying to stop me, which would force me to fight you!"

The woman hurried back to her desk and took up the phone to warn her boss. By the time it rang, Rochelle was banging on the door. Cathie dragged it open unexpectedly. When she came face to face with the venomous wife she made a muffled shriek and tried reclosing it. Rochelle pushed by and went inside.

Cathie was shaking.

"I need your help! Benny only listens to you!"

Cathie calmed down feeling proud about what she heard. Rochelle said the truth. He was in pain. She was there for him! She inherited influence over him!

"OK, Rochelle," she agreed, "But I am on his side where ever there is contention between both of you. I'm sorry to say that!"

"I understand. There's no contention at all! I need you to do something for me...for *him*!"

"If it will help him then I am in whole-heartedly."

"Thanks Cathie." She paused, trying not to, but then she had to ask, "Have I lost him yet?"

"No. But I believe you chose to not have him."

Rochelle ignored her. "Am I in danger of losing him?"

Cathie stiffened and then froze. She mustered the courage and replied, "What if you don't like the answer? You do have a reputation for fighting!"

"Those women were stalking him against his will. I never fought Betsy Frazier. Why would I fight you?"

"Oh, I get it. I never thought about it that way!"

"I'm ever misunderstood! Tell me, are you a threat?"

"Who in her right mind wouldn't want him Rochelle?"

"Silly me!" Rochelle said sadly. Cathie understood her. She could not help with that one.

"You make me feel bad about me, Rochelle. Now that you exposed the bitch in me, let us get to what you came about!"

"What I came about is impossible to believe!"

"I'm the woman who believes Benny's impossible story, remember?"

"Well I'm a believer now! When I show you this video, you can pat yourself on the back!"

....

At the end of the second week, the hearing was just around the corner. She advised Benny to make the payment but he was as stubborn as ever. It seemed he expected some divine force to suddenly appear and absolve him. He saw the whole thing as fraud and extortion. He was working to go to jail!

Finding her was easy. She lived in an apartment complex but the apartments were in moderately poor condition. Cathie drove by the residents parking area looking for number 05. When she identified the slot she drove to the visitors parking area to watch from inside her car.

She was not home. Fay told Rochelle that Betsy would be off that day. Her car was not in the parking area. She thought about calling Rochelle but changed her mind and waited.

In less than a minute, the old 323 Mazda drove up and filled the spot.

Betsy switched off the engine and leaned back inside the car. Then she closed her eyes to dream, saying, "Oh,

Bentley my son, you'll be a rich boy soon! No more old worn out cars – and you'll live in a decent hou…"

She heard the car door slam shut and stopped talking. Bentley had jumped out of the car. He charged up the steps and stood to wait for her. Betsy hustled after him, "Bentley! You better mind your manners boy! I was talking to you! Do you want more spanking?"

"*Ma'am!*" someone called from her right. She stopped in her tracks to see Cathie hustling to her with a cell phone in her hand. "I'm sorry! You don't know me but I need…" Cathie froze in mocked disbelief and then said excitedly, "Oh my God! It's you! You're Benny Benson's boy's mom! You're famous!"

Betsy smiled with pride, feeding on the excitement, "Yes. It's me," she reported.

Cathie caught hold of herself in a conspicuous way. "I was so thrilled to meet you I forgot my problem!"

"It'll come back my dear?" Betsy offered, feeling well fed by Cathie's adoration.

"*Oh*! My phone went dead and I have to call my uncle at River's Valley!"

Betsy shuffled in the side of her hand bag and said, "You seem like a nice lady! Use mine!"

"Gee! Thanks!" She called her house number and then declared that no one was picking up. "I guess I have to sit in my car and wait. I might come and get your phone to try again though – If you don't mind. Someone will get back soon to pick up the call."

"Sure! I don't mind! You can wait inside my house. Then you won't have to come knocking at the door!"

"Wow! Thank you! You are so wonderful! Some celebrities are not!"

Betsy smiled at the realization that she was now a celebrity. "When we get inside," she offered, "I will show you some beautiful pictures of me training my baby Benny to run. He is fast like Usain Bolt!"

"Awesome! They say Benny Benson never looked at another woman but Rochelle before you. How on earth did you manage to get in? That must be the heights of girl power! You have to teach other girls the trick!"

Betsy giggled and did the awful walk. "*I know!*"

Cathie took out her phone again as she followed the old princess. She cleared the screen, opened the app, and put it in her handbag....

9

When the bailiff called the court to order Benny's heart rose to his throat. This was it! He thought he did not care but now he did! This was what he was getting for not accepting a lie!

Attorney Barnaby was half-heartedly going through the motions yesterday. He seemed happy today! Today it would be over for him either way. Benny could not fault the guy! He did all he could but his stubborn client would not act on advice! As everyone else, he thought the big athlete was impossible! Benny refused to pay support for a child he did not bring into this world!

Whatever con game Betsy Frazier came with would not work with the Flash of the West Keyes Island.

The attorney seemed enthusiastic and confident this morning! When you consider the uphill task he got, he was a commendable liar. Outside of court he tried his best to convince Benny to tell the truth and work from there. In court he insisted that he believed every word that Benny said. Some people would swear that living by being a liar was honorable.

Benny glanced at Betsy and Sobers and saw the contrast! They skinned their teeth waiting for the New Jerusalem. Benny Benson money would rain on them soon – Today or in the very near future. He did not pay up in three weeks but they were certain that he would. He would not make it easy for them! He could even go to jail too – So there!

Still, Benny did not want to be locked up especially with young Benny to think about. He could not handle it and with the stories about what could happen in there! No, he would pay but at the very last possible second! All along he hoped that some miraculous twist would bring out the truth before it got this far. It never happened. He let go off that impossible hope.

Rochelle came! That was shocking! He wished she stayed home. He believed she would watch him suffer and salt the wounds as usual! For the first time in all his pains she was in court on his side, waving support. If one miracle could happen the other could happen too!

Everyone, even those with excuse to not be there the last time, was in court today. Rochelle's parents sat behind her bench. His parents sat on the left of Rochelle, like they owned her as usual! It was his dad's first trip – when it was too late! He turned to face the devil and forget about futile support.

Another thought struck him. He frowned and looked around! Cathie sat at Rochelle's right hand! How could that happen? How many times had he dreamt that poor Cathie went through First Lady Venomous' shredder? Now they smiled and talked with each other! What more miracles could happen in a day?

A nice looking lady sat beside Cathie. She was familiar but he could not recall where he met her. He remembered wondering if Rochelle took negative to him admiring her. She was a magnetic being who drew you in. Rochelle took all for a threat, including innocent compliments. Her philosophy was *'nip it in the bud'*. After all the nipping, Betsy Frazier and that Bentley kid still came! She and the entire world were blaming him!

He looked to the contrast again. The look of impatience was conspicuous on Milton Sobers face. He wanted to be rich off this one. Benny was the only none-smiling face! Maybe his family wanted to send him to jail and get it over with for a lie he did not tell.

Judge Maria Mason spoke directly to Betsy Frazier, "Miss Frazier."

"Yes, Your Honor. It is me!"

"I am sure that it is you! This should be your big day. Are you excited?"

"Yes I am, Your Honor! Bentley will finally get his father and his legacy. And I will finally get my Benny when *she* divorces him. So..."

Sobers nudged Betsy with his elbow and she stopped. Maria Mason smiled, "Do not worry Mr. Sobers – My bad! I believe that all of us here were ignoring most of those unnecessary comments anyway. I asked if she was excited…I expected 'yes' or 'no'!"

She took off her glasses, wiped it and returned it to her face. Then she looked at Benny until he felt uncomfortable. Finally, she offered, "Mr. Benny Benson, the hero of West Keyes and the hero of this court today. I hardly slept last night because of you! You are a very strong character – Do you know that?"

"Yes Your Honor." He said and then added sarcastically, "I stand up for what I believe in!"

"As long as that concept is not 'misplaced' it is usually an honorable trait. Are you ready for an extremely complicated day? I prepared for it for days, asking advice and looking for advisors. I still don't know that I found the solution! At first, it seemed simple! Suddenly everything changed! Bare your knuckles my son! I think the playing field is now level. You now have a fair fight! Are you sure you are ready for it?"

"Whatever comes Your Honor!"

"Why do you look so sad! Your situation improved!"

Attorney Barnaby reached over to touch Benny on his shoulder, smiling. "He still doesn't have a clue, Your Honor! No one told him!"

"*Why*?" The judge asked and Milton Sobers asked "*What*?" simultaneously.

"Mr. Sobers," the judge offered, "We got new compelling information at the last minute, which I am about to inform you and the defendant who has not heard as yet either."

"What new evidence can better a paternity test and give him an advantage, Your Honor? That is impossible." Milton Sobers spoke, smiling with confidence.

"Who said that anything 'bettered' a paternity test? I am saying that it changes the perspectives A LOT. At least for example, when it comes to retroactive child support payments, attorney fees and other damages. When it comes to child support, we are confused! That is putting it mildly!"

"If the defendant puts forward any new evidence that will affect the court decisions today, then it is only fair that we have time to look over it, Your Honor!"

"No one had time Mr. Sobers. The defendant does not know what we are talking about! I do not see what could possibly make it inadmissible either. I am supposed to make decisions. Your looking over anything is not going to affect how I think, even if you get an extra twenty years to do so! We will look together today, debate together today and then I will make decisions! I will not do it on another day! This case is killing me!"

Sobers swallowed hard and said, "Whatever it is cannot hurt our case. I am ready too, Your Honor!"

"Good I enjoyed this part! Let us get to business!"

She paused watching Benny with intent. Finally she said, "I am having a problem to begin, Mr. Benson. I do not know how prepared I am for this. I invited some people to come and assist us when we need it."

She took off her glasses and wiped it off. Then she turned to Betsy's attorney, "Mr. Sobers, I hope you can answer the questions I have for Mrs. Frazier. We are in court! She will remember swearing to tell the truth!"

"My client understands quite well, Your Honor," Sobers said with confidence, "We have no problems clearing up any issue so that we can get on with the matter of payment and reimbursement."

"Good! Now let me ask you this again. How did Mrs. Frazier meet Mr. Benson?"

"She met him at the Clair-Castle Hotel on…"

"I get that, but where inside the hotel did they meet – inside the room or outside…Give me specifics!"

"Well, they first met in the corridor of…"

"And did he have sex with her?"

"Obviously and unquestionably *yes* Your Honor!"

She put her glasses back on and looked under the rim at Betsy. "Is that right Mrs. Frazier. Did you have sex with Benny Benson?"

"I had sex, Your Honor!"

"Where did you have sex?"

"In my Benny's room!"

"And where was Rochelle Benson at the time?"

Betsy paused to think. Then she said, "It's a long time ago, Your Honor. I cannot remember quite clearly."

"Fine! But do you remember actually having sex with Mr. Benson? Did he invite you to his room?"

"How else could it be, Your Honor? You have the test results!" Milton chipped in.

"I am not trying to find out if Bentley is Mr. Benson's child. We know that for sure!"

Sobers affirmed, "We already have the most important evidence! The other questions are irrelevant. They had sex and they produced a child, Your Honor!"

"Not so fast, dude!" Judge Mason declared jovially with an ace, "You don't get away with this! The questions I ask will be relevant in how I make my judgment later on! I have at least two witnesses, plus other substantial evidence to say that Mr. Benson did not know Miss Betsy, even though she was pregnant with his child! If we have to, we might even go to Miss Betsy's confession against Miss Betsy!"

Sobers tore his eyes open and looked at the judge incredulously, "That is not possible, Your Honor. How could he have sex with her if he did not know her?"

"Wrong again Mr. Sobers! What makes my information so relevant is the fact that it proposes that Betsy Frazier did not have sex with Mr. Benson!"

Mr. Sobers held his hands on top of his head and moaned like a man in pain. Betsy watched the judge nervously, still too dazed to take in all that transpired.

"Now I have your attention!" Maria Mason declared triumphantly. "This is where our first witness comes in! Mrs. Frazier has a minute to tell us anything that may have been omitted before we get to that! I doubt that whatever she says today will make much difference either way. I will warn you all. I already made decisions. There is hardly a case left to try! I only offer an opportunity for anyone on a sinking ship to come up with the miracle of salvation."

Neither Betsy nor Sobers took up on the offer, so Judge Mason turned to speak to Benny, who simply fainted! This time, Rochelle flew from where she was sitting and collided with Cathie who was rushing to him too! Attorney Barnaby was now an expert at re-awakening him. He had to fight off Betsy Frazier for the space to do so.

"Poor fellow!" Maria Mason lamented, "He's under so much pressure!" Rochelle and Cathie were still scrambling to come over and she assured them, "Hold your seats! These men are experts at this by now!"

Benny rose lazily. "Are you ready now Mr. Benson?"

"Yes, Your Honor."

"Are you sure?"

"Yes Your Honor."

"Sorry I shocked you! It came as a shock to me too!"

"I enjoyed being shocked Your Honor!"

"I imagine that!" She pointed to the audience and said, "Please come forward Miss Ambrose!"

Betsy Frazier spun on a dime and saw her! Fay caught her eyes and smiled cheekily.

"Jesus Christ!" Betsy declared, "Don't let this witch tell lies! *Bitch*, what are you doing here? This is my case! You should be at work!"

Maria Mason smiled, allowing Betsy to vent. Fay approached the bench.

"*Bitch*!" Betsy repeated, "I want my car back!"

"What is it about a car? And what about that B word in my court?" The Judge asked.

"She gave me a car one day Your Honor. I'm trying not to remember what it was for!"

"It was to keep your mouth shut!" Betsy declared in ignorance. Maria Mason's mouth sagged open. Crazy Fay giggled. "I traded it in Your Honor. It got old."

"So you broke your oath?"

"Never Your Honor! I promised not to tell Jennifer and Cassandra who are not in court today!"

"Which means you will tell us – Right?"

"Right, Your Honor! Hallelujah! I'm so glad to tell!" She giggled and grinned at the judge, showing strong white rows of teeth. Maria Mason's immediate adoration for this happy go lucky woman was evident.

"You are a little devil Miss Fay Ambrose! I like you!"

"Thanks Your Honor. I do my devil best!"

"OK, Miss Ambrose, I hope the devil does not mind swearing on the Bible. It is that time now. You will take your oath and then tell us the story!"

"Fine Your Honor! Just don't give me any loop holes! You saw what it did to Betsy!"

Maria Mason cackled, "There is no loophole my child! I have a remedy for any contempt of this court! If you want to test it be my guess!"

Fay muffed a giggle and shrugged off her show of bravado. Mario took off her glasses and inspected her deliberately. When she was satisfied she sat up straight, put her glasses back on and said, "I guess that you're settled now. Are you ready to be a good girl?"

"Yes Your Honor!" Fay offered hastily, muffing out another involuntary giggle attack.

After Fay got sworn in, Judge Maria addressed them again. "I warn you all! This case is not normal! There are no unconventional ways to deal with court matters. We will settle the obvious here, today! However, there will likely come a time when I could make you an offer to sit as a mediator so we can iron out and settle other grievances. It will be up to you all to decide."

She paused, wiped her glasses and eyed the stumpy attorney. "Mr. Sobers, you've been anxious to see the settlement in cash for retroactive payments, child support and other damages you're trying to convince us about. You will be happy to know that the question of child support will be settled today. There is no doubt that Mr. Benson will be asked to take responsibility for his son!"

Betsy screamed *"Hallelujah!"* and held up her right hand to God. Sobers eyed her with a half-satisfied smile. That was not the meaty part to him!

Maria added, "The senior Bensons filed for custody of Bentley! They are keeping the child safe until the question of Miss Betsy's sanity is revealed! There are some damning claims against her, both from Bentley and her own lips! We will go through them briefly. For now, Mr. Benson cannot pay support for a child in his custody. Mr. Benson will pay for the three weeks since our last hearing and since the paternity test confirmed that he was the father. I will not hold him responsible for the period when he did not know about a child!"

"Objection Your Honor!" Milton interrupted.

"Yes?" the judge asked seemingly irritated.

"The fact is that he knew about the child and refused to…"

"Shut up Mr. Sobers! That has come into question! I am sure Miss Frazier will not want Miss Cathie to come and refute that! I will speak to the fact that he is the father. Not to claims that might be debunked before we are through! Here is another likely scenario. Short of a miracle, all cost including lawyer fees will be Miss Frazier's liability. That will include Mr. Benson's cost to his lawyer."

Sobers opened his mouth to question but refrained from talking. He looked to Fay, waiting for answers. Betsy screamed hysterically, "No Your Honor! Get that woman out of here! And send that Cathie home too! They planned lies!"

Fay giggled and it was contagious. The judge stifled one of her own.

Maria continued, "If Mr. Benson takes custody of Bentley, it would help the court make its best decision.

We recommend that Miss Betsy Frazier receives the necessary psychological evaluation as early as possible. In the mean time, we want to know that the child is properly secured. It is in Bentley's best interest to stay with his grandmother, who has already declared her availability until we settle this matter!"

She paused and eyed all the stake holders for questions. No one spoke. "However, Mr. Sobers, we will not settle the question of other payments today or any other day. Mr. Benson owes no one anything and the witness on the stand is only the icing on the cake of how I came to my decisions! On the contrary though, Mr. Benson is bent on countersuing for a load of damages! That is why I offer you my free service as a mediator to settle these differences without wasting the court's time! All that I say now will become clear to Mr. Sobers in a few minutes. I am sure Miss Betsy already knows of her own doings!"

Mr. Sobers seemed puzzled but he refrained from speaking and waited for the revelations to come. Benny was not used to good favor in court. He almost fainted again! Attorney Barnaby looked unperturbed. Benny took a glance at Rochelle. She smiled warmly back at him. What the heck was going on? Fay muffed a giggle.

"Question anyone? Speak before we proceed!" Maria watched them. She had on a knowing smile. They were more anxious to listen than to speak at that point.

....

Clair-Castle room count was over ninety percent. More than three thousand guests reported for breakfast. It was a busy day. Too many workers found time to be in the cafeteria on working hours.

Jennifer and Cassandra were on split shift. They were done for the morning. Being caught up in the case, they decided to sit out the time in the cafeteria and then work their afternoon shift instead of going home.

Jennifer looked around and said "Seems like everyone is inside here! Doesn't anyone have work to do?"

Cassandra laughed, "No one wants to miss this Jennifer! Most people will be in for a shocker today!"

"Yes! I was shocked to see all our coworkers cheering for the wicked bitch! They'll have egg on their faces later! Poor Benny Benson!"

"Poor Benny Benson! He's such a great guy. I wish he could sue for damages but that wouldn't even make sense – would it?"

"Wouldn't make sense! She couldn't pay for shit. At least he could still sue for *freaky* rape!"

"That's a new one!"

They went silent for a minute. Cassandra said, "Fay and her giggling! Nothing makes her nervous!"

"I wish I had her confidence. She always feels like everything will be fine. It's her personality!"

"I always tell you to take a leaf from her book. You worry too god damned much!"

"I can't help it! But she's being rude - *ish* and that judge likes her for it. She'd throw *me* in jail!"

"It's what I try to tell you! You need confidence! That judge understands her. I only wish we could be there!"

"Me too! She looks so good in her clothes. She must thank you for dressing her Cassandra."

"I only made suggestions. She would be on TV - so. She can thank me with some of the thank you money that Benny will give her!"

"Fay isn't doing it for money. She just wants to help! Why do you think they're going to…?"

"What would you do if you were in the Bensons' position and someone appeared with *'salvation'*?"

Jennifer thought. "Oh gee! I'd give her so much money she'd stop working!"

"There you have it!"

"But most rich people don't give a shit though!"

"That's true but we'll see. For now we'll watch Fay make use of her fifteen minutes of fame! She's the star out there!"

Jennifer would speak again but Fay finished swearing in. She took the stand. They froze. It seemed they did not even allow breathing to take place.

Maria Mason said, *"The stand is yours Miss Ambrose. Go back to that day nine years ago when it all began. Tell us in details what you saw. Giggle a bit but not much and make sure to tell only the truth! You're under oath my child. Make Mr. Sobers see clearly!"*

Fay saw Betsy's angry face telegraphing a threat to her. She found it to be more funny than intimidating.

"Someone might have to pay for a car!" Betsy muttered beneath her breath but audibly enough.

Judge Mason turned to her. *"What did you say Miss Betsy? Tell me and then I will ask you to keep quiet or face the consequences!"*

Sobers flashed an eye to quiet Betsy. He turned to the judge and said, *"It's OK Your Honor. My client was venting grievances that are personal and have nothing to do with this case. I apologize to the court. I am sure she will restrain herself from henceforth."*

Maria Mason wiped her glasses and then spoke. *"I doubt everything you just said Mr. Sobers. I am still quite curious but I will let it slide for now!"*

Fay muffled a giggle again, *"Can I anxiously speak light to your curiosity Your Honor?"*

"Great! I love your enthusiasm! By all means, go ahead and enlighten me!"

"I heard what she said about a car Your Honor. That will come in the last part of my statement here."

"Very well! Give us all the sweet juicy details!"

"Please be cautious about those words you use Your Honor! There are things that are sweet and juicy. This is very unpalatable! Be warned that anyone in here might feel compelled to throw up at any time! Please do not hold me responsible! You asked for 'details'!"

The entire cafeteria burst out in cheering and laughing for their coworker's bravado in the court.

"You have a respectful impolite sweetness that I have never seen Miss Ambrose. Carry on! We'll handle it!"

"No Your Honor! She's not sweet!" Betsy raged, "She's lying! We can't handle it! Tell her not to speak!"

"It's alright Miss Betsy," the judge assured her, "We love to hear Miss Ambrose speak! She's not the only one who will speak today. I must inform you that Miss Cathie Crew has something to say too!"

"She'll only tell lies that she can't prove!"

....

Inside the court, Judge Mason sat staring drop jawed into space. Fay watched her and giggled. Maria did not handle it well! Everyone but Rochelle, Catherine and attorney Barnaby were in inconceivable awe.

Benny fainted. This time Betsy did not move to him. Rochelle and Catherine rose simultaneously. Barnaby waved to tell them that he would take care of it.

Fay looked at the judge and giggled again. Maria Mason returned to reality and took off her glasses. She began to wipe them off.

"Must I continue now Your Honor?" Fay asked.

The judge winced, "Sure go ahead but take it easy. Try to find words to spare me the full blunt! Please don't kill me my dear!"

Judge Mason watched Betsy with befuddling intent. Betsy watched everywhere else to avoid her attention. The magistrate said, "Suddenly, the *'baby I'm still a virgin'* comment pops to my mind!"

That comment seemed to turn on a light bulb in the room. Everyone suddenly declared the revelations.

Fay watched Benny nervously. He got to his feet and seemed alright. She continued, "So I took the car Keyes from her. She signed over the title that evening. I thought that there was no way anyone could get hurt by it, so I did her the favor and kept my mouth shut. Then *this*! Who on earth would think it could happen? When she spoke out of turn earlier she told me to pay for the car. She thinks that I breached the agreement. I think Miss Betsy will sue me!"

"Did you have a written confidentiality contract?"

"No Your Honor. I..."

"Oh, I knew you don't! I'm just saying that to expose a futile premise! Giggle and carry on Miss Ambrose!"

"I did not breach the agreement! I didn't tell the two people she told me not to tell!"

"I know. You said that earlier. And all you're saying now could seal my judgment if someone on the other side doesn't come better!"

Sobers butted in, "I'll come better Your Honor! Miss Ambrose's story is nonsense! When has there been any precedence of this thing happening? How can it be possible? The semen would have died on contact with the spermicidal agent inside of the condom. Moreover, even without that poison, the sperms would die minutes after being ejaculated. This is impossible! It has never and will never happen! Let us put this little fairy tale to rest and ask Mr. Benson to pay over what he owes this woman whom he has taken advantage of!"

"Wow!" Maria mused, "You are the doctor now? Thank you for enlightening us! Now, let us hear from a real scientist!"

Judge Maria Mason called the biologist Dr. Danville Graham to the stand to verify the credibility of Fay's story. The doctor swore in and sat beside the witness.

"Dr. Graham, you heard what Mr. Sobers said. If you could just comment on that alone we would be done with the issue."

"Sure Your Honor! Mr. Sobers said there has never been any precedence to this matter. He is wrong. It happened before. It is not common but it happened more than a few times. Men have been forced to accept paternity for children that they had no choice in deciding to bring into the world. On the matter of *'spermicidal agents'* the following is true. Not every condom carries a substance that will kill the sperms. Even in cases where they do, some sperms can likely survive long enough to fertilize an egg within the space of a few minutes of being ejaculated into the condom."

"Well!" Maria said, "The bigger doctor has spoken! We know where we're going from here!"

"No Your Honor!" Betsy chipped. "Don't go that way! They're telling impossible lies? The bathroom door was locked! She did not see me do it! She could not!"

Judge Mason replied in disgust, "Well it's your word against hers then Miss Betsy. Are we having a standoff, or is someone going to come clean?"

"It's not my word against hers Your Honor!" Fay injected, "It's my Galaxy against her words!"

Maria took off her glasses again and frowned. "What?"

Betsy tried to storm Fay to grab the phone. "Jesus Christ Your Honor! Don't let her show you that thing! I refuse to be on a video! It is against my human rights! *Bitch*! When I said delete I meant to delete it!"

Two police officers came and restrained her. Fay giggled and asked, "Do you have a Galaxy Your Honor!"

"No child, I never tried one before. My daughter and husband do though. I believe Miss Cathie Crew has the latest version!"

"I strongly recommend it! You can buy one at Haddo's today!"

"Great ad, but right now I have to grab yours!"

Maria Mason took the phone and addressed Betsy, simultaneously, "This video might end up in the hands of the media before we're done in here!"

She started watching. She froze. Her face turned to the perfect image of horror. "Oh, my goodness!" she lamented. "This is not easy Mr. Benson! Now I understand why you would faint! Please. Pass this around for all concerned to see! Don't show Mr. Benson unless he asks! He won't handle it well!"

"I don't wana see it!" Betsy declared stubbornly.

"That's alright Miss Frazier. You created the act. You need not see it to believe it anymore!" she paused and then added, "And the thing that really gets me is how you profane the flag of our beautiful land! Look at the length of that pole! How on earth did you pull that off? It kills me!"

Fay winced and closed her eyes tight, trying to forget the depth that shaft was inserted inside Betsy while she cooed and called Benny Benson's name in wishful bliss.

Sobers saw the video and turned to Betsy, "*Seriously*? Woman you fucked me up!"

He fainted. Maria slapped down the hammer to throw him out for misconduct. Two police officers came to lift him out. She slapped down the hammer again to dismiss the case against Benny Benson.

Cathie went to Benny, "Congratulations my friend!"

"Thanks Cathie! Thanks to you! It's not even over yet! I'm going to get my own against that tramp! She raped my sperm! She stole my property!"

"I know!" Cathie saw Rochelle coming. She stepped away and waited in a corner.

Rochelle came to him looking awkward, "Congratulations Benny."

"Thank you Rochelle. I appreciate you coming."

"I owe you a thousand apologies! I'm so sorry!"

"Yeah! You're right and wrong at the same time!"

"*I know*!" She paused and then said, "Are you coming home tonight?"

"I don't know. I need some time." He glanced over his shoulder to where Cathie stood. Rochelle saw her waiting and conceded.

"I see. I hope you'll call me and let me know what you'll do from here."

"I will. Definitely!"

"What about Bentley? What are you planning to do?"

"A lot for him. A lot with him…cause now I know he's really my child…"

"I'm thrilled to hear that!"

"God I really want to legally get at that woman's throat!"

"Take Bentley! That'll kill her! Are you going to set up the hearing with the judge as mediator?"

"Yes! I don't want her money…well…she has none but I want her to feel some stress!"

Rochelle cupped her hands on her face. "Gee! When you say that it only reminds me of my own bad against you! I wish I could take it all back."

She was waiting for him to respond but then he said, "I better be going," and went to Cathie.

10

She mustered the courage and went to knock on his door. He answered on the third call and she asked, "Were you asleep Benny?"

"No. I was watching West Keyes Spotlight."

"Oh."

"Why?"

"Do you feel like talking?" she asked hoarsely.

"Come in Cathie."

She pushed the door and walked inside looking freaked out. He was resting on his back in bed watching the TV. She was tripping, looking for a nonexistent chair to sit on. He knocked the side of the bed. She went cautiously to sit beside him.

"Can I say something to you Benny? It is only right to speak my mind."

"Speak or forever hold your peace," he advised with a jolly chuckle.

"Alright!" she said and then paused. He watched her. Cathie seemed fearful. Finally, she said "Benny!"

"Hmm?"

"I have a crush on you and it's very big...and painful!"

"Cathie, I know! We both like each other! But..."

As he said 'but' she quickly put her finger on his lips. He stopped. "I understand," she offered. "Do me a favor. Kiss my lips before you say no!"

He leaned over and kissed her lips. Then they watched TV together.

"She was your best friend, wasn't she?"

"She was. She's still somewhere in here," he touched his heart. "She made it hard to find her there lately. What you did for me I expected from her!"

"I'm not better than her. I won't put her down to get you. There is no way to say she was wrong. I got the vision this time around. That's all! She's a good wife for you. I would rather it be me but stay where you are!"

"Please Cathie, don't talk! When you talk I know you better and it doesn't help! You're simply awesome!"

"Alright, *friend*! Let's watch TV!"

As if they would not guess, Benny Benson was one of two topics on the talk show that evening. The other was about whether West Keyes needed a real army.

One man said. "Some small countries have first world armies! We have armies in the Caribbean. Everyone knows about the superior force of Cuba. Jamaica has a good Army! They have real soldiers Aubrey! Put a Jamaican sniper in the US Marines and he would not be a fish out of water. Jamaican soldiers are trained to pull their weight in the world. They don't have much to spend on equipment! We have money but what do we have in way of a security force? School cadets! That's what we have! Send our Army leader to cadet school in

America and they would have to train him from the elementary stage!"

"It's not like we're fighting wars - Is it?"

"Everyone will have a battle at some time. If it's even against an internal force!"

"Ah crap! There's nothing to fight over in the Caribbean!"

"Says who Duane? Last time I went to Trinidad they were fighting with Barbados all day over flying fish! Barbados has to defend their fish borders against a Trinidad force that can blow them out of the fucking water like abracadabra!"

"Is Flying Fish the national dish of Barbados?"

"Actually, it's Flying Fish and Coo-Coo."

"*What*? You're joking right? Or is Coo-Coo, in this case, different from what the word suggests?"

"Coo-Coo is a fine meal. Not what *you* think the word suggests Aubrey. I must admit that there is a bit of *the other* coo-coo in it! I mean, who fights over flying fish?"

"People fight over everything Duane! We are no different from Trinidad and Barbados! Don't forget our fishermen claim Jamaicans are fishing up conk from our waters. It's getting heated out there! Soon you might be asking who fights over conk meat."

"That brings me back to the question of national security. Suppose we decide to fight over conk meat? One canoe load of Jamaican gangsters could come here and colonize this country! We couldn't do a damned thing about it! Unless we give extortion money to some Trinidadian bad boys to protect us! We're helpless!"

"Oh come on Duane! It's not so bad!"

"What's not so bad? Our national security is inept! It only took one half docile woman to rape the West Keyes flag! She buried a foot of an eighteen inch flag pole! Six puny inches! That's all we had left!"

Aubrey chuckled with restraint. "On that disgusting topic! The woman is a serial rapist! She literally raped and impregnated a man in his absence! Look deep and see how she raped his innocence and integrity! He was guilty of fathering the boy. How do you get around it?"

"Imagine the hell he went through. He can't be satisfied with the outcome yet. For a space in time, he was the extreme devil. The world and his wife were hell bent on sending him to hell in his innocence!"

"Considering the facts that were out there, could you blame anyone? Were you thinking any different from what Rochelle Benson was thinking?"

"No Aubrey! I'm stomped right there! This woman had Benny by the wrong body part! Is there any way he could get more justice than a simple exoneration?"

"He got custody of the child. That's heavy on Betsy!"

"But is that enough Aubrey? Would you be satisfied with the outcome? Wouldn't you want to see that woman pay more?"

"Pay with what Duane? Maybe he could sue for damages but would that help?"

"It would help to the degree that it puts put her back through the shredder Aubrey!"

"You have a point. Could he charge her for rape?"

"I wondered the same thing Duane! Benny was protecting the sanctity of his marriage. It wasn't his doing but an outside child came into their lives. Could Rochelle charge Betsy for the rape of her union? Technically she raped and framed her too! She also made her the unwitting accomplice!"

"Well in my court that's two counts of rape Aubrey!"

"How about adultery? Who would we say committed it? Surely not Benny or Rochelle!"

"I get you Aubrey. Here is how I would interpret it in my court. You know like when you deliberately pass on a sexually transmitted disease?"

"Yes Duane."

"So I would interpret it as she giving him a case of adultery. She could be charged and he could sue!"

Aubrey laughed, "You should become a law maker!"

"Oh, I'm ready for it. Any other case?"

"I have one that will bowl you over!"

"Try me nut head!"

"What about the fact that she stole his property from the condom? How would you interpret it?"

"*Nope!*"

"What do you mean by nope Duane?"

"I mean 'nope' there's no charge for stolen property. That property was in the dumps and free for all! Plus, she was the person it was left there for to cleanup."

"And that's where I got you! Now you're making her go scotch free for the injustice Duane!"

"*Nope!* Finding a condom, inserting semen from it, or doing gymnastics with it is no injustice to any third party. It is injustice to one's self!"

"I can't figure you out! Now she has a right to ask for retroactive support and all the works – Huh?"

"*Nope!* Listen to my law! If you find an old phone marked Motorola in a trash can then that phone could be yours. You have a right to use it. However, if you want to use that phone, with that phone name to start a company named Motorola, using the technology on that phone named Motorola then all the fraud and theft charges will be laid against you! That law stands in Betsy Frazier's case. She infringed on someone else's trademark, making a product in the name of that trademark and demanding payment as owner for copyright based on that trademark!"

"You're stark crazy pal!" Duane mused. "Let's go straight to the phones! Let the people of West Keyes call and say how crazy you are! Hello listeners! Please call and let us know if you agree with the Laws of

Aubrey – Or just go ahead and propose the laws yourself! What will you charge Betsy Frazier for to get justice for Benny Benson?"

....

Three weeks later…

Sunday morning she rose early to horns honking in her yard. Cathie peeped through the window and saw the BMW. She hurried down to see what the surprise visitor wanted.

When she pushed the door Rochelle was standing beside her car. Even though it was Cathie's home, the woman looked surprised to see her there. She scanned the pretty woman in her night dress and lost her tongue. Cathie's beauty made her nervous!

Cathie saw her uneasiness. "Hi Rochelle!"

She paused. Rochelle made to speak but stopped.

"OK." Cathie offered awkwardly, "I'll get him up!"

She turned and went back through the door. When she was inside she heard Rochelle say. "Thanks."

She went upstairs and knocked him up. Benny came out of his room inspecting her from top to bottom. She grabbed him suddenly and kissed him. He pulled back in shock and she said, "Go! Downstairs! Just go! Hurry! I'll bring your belongings!"

When Cathie came back down with his stuff, he was in his car and she stood beside her BMW waiting. She rested the stuff down and held her hand out to Rochelle. "Here's all his stuff and there's all of him! I want you to know so you'll make no mistake next time!"

Rochelle took the handshake and then turned it into an embrace. "Thank you sister! Thank you so much! This boy sure knows how to pick his women and that shit makes me damned scared! I was such a fool!"

"You know you're no fool so stop it! What happened could deceive the very elect!"

"It did not fool you!"

"Sometimes we're lucky, we fall through the crack! He has an age old friendship with you. It goes beyond your marriage and he cherishes it. If not for that I could have gotten in."

"He would be in good hands anyway. I could not live down my mistake."

Suddenly, Sobers drove Betsy's Mazda car into the yard!

Benny hopped out of his vehicle and watched in dismay. "Mr. Benson!" Sobers began, this time in a friendly way. Betsy Frazier was getting out of the car!

Cathie put her hands on top of her head and lamented, *"Oh Jesus*!"

The stubby man walked up to Benny, "The grapevine said that I'd find you here! Unfortunately, the two women are here as well!"

"Don't let me start throwing people out of my yard!" Cathie warned, annoyed at his insinuations.

"But wait!" he replied hastily. "I am not here to judge! This is important!"

"So," Benny said matter-of-factually. "She's bribing you with a car today. Does she ever learn from past mistakes?"

"Come on Mr. Benson! Let bygones be bygones! I'm only here to propose that you take it easy on her! Betsy needs to at least have weekends with the boy! You're the only one who can help! Don't be bad about this! It's about the child! He'll need both his parents!"

"The boy doesn't want to be near her! I can't force him on a parent he doesn't want to see! I'm enjoying the ruling! The court thinks Bentley is not safe around her. I agree! You want to endanger my child in order to keep a Mazda car? Is that what you want Mr. Sobers?"

"Oh come on man!" Sobers pleaded.

Cathie was about to speak but then she eyed Rochelle and kept her silent. Rochelle saw Cathie's reaction and chipped in, "That is enough! My husband has had it with you! Get out of here before it's too late! I'll make sure there is a restraining order against this Olive Oil and this knit-wit attorney! Leave my husband alone!"

As Rochelle spoke Benny stepped to Sobers. Cathie smiled watching the chubby man back off. Betsy came forward screaming "No, no, noooo! This isn't over!"

Rochelle growled lustfully and stepped to her, expertly grabbing a shoe from her left foot in the same motion. Benny held her elbow and pulled her back.

"*Rochelle* – Don't honey!" he pleaded with urgency. Rochelle's eyes brightened at how he spoke to her. She listened to him and relaxed.

Then Betsy said "So Benny, what about my tattoos honey? I'm crying and you don't even notice me!"

Rochelle stiffened and made to take the offensive. She eyed Benny and calmed down. "Clear off!" she snapped at the wiry woman.

"Your name's not Benny! I'm not talking to you!"

"My name is Mrs. Benny Benson *bitch*! If I hear another peep out of you I'll break you all over!"

Betsy stepped back timidly. She held onto the car door to prepare for a hasty retreat.

"Go talk to him Mr. Sobers! Convince him and get this car!"

Sobers stepped forth to convince him and get the car.

"And you, Penguin," Benny advised, adding to his wife's violent threat, "go back to Goddamned City!"

"Yes!" Rochelle hissed gleefully in support, "Go back to Goddamned City!"

....and then they lived happily ever after.

....

Sobers charged Betsy the price of the car for his fee. She had no money so he took the car.

Betsy Frazier took a boat, a train and then a plane to Jamaica to find Usain St. Leo Bolt.

She determined to name the next child *St. Leo Usain Bolt* and **BOOM**, she would be rich!

The end...

In the mean time, here's a warning for you!
Be careful how you use toilet paper!
*The details will come in "***Immaculate Contention***", by* **Mark Flame** *the brain of the game.*
Look out for it!